THE INHERITANCE OF WORDS

From the Jungle Series
Bhanu Tatak

THE INHERITANCE
OF WORDS

Writings from Arunachal Pradesh

MAMANG DAI
Editor

zubaan

ZUBAAN
128 B Shahpur Jat, 1st Floor
New Delhi 110 049
Website: www.zubaanbooks.com
Email: contact@zubaanbooks.com

First published in hardback by Zubaan Publishers Pvt. Ltd, 2021

Published in association with the Sasakawa Peace Foundation

10 9 8 7 6 5 4 3 2 1

ISBN 978 81 94760 53 5
eBook ISBN 978 81 94760 54 2

Zubaan is an independent feminist publishing house based in New Delhi with a strong academic and general list. It was set up as an imprint of India's first feminist publishing house, Kali for Women, and carries forward Kali's tradition of publishing world-quality books to high editorial and production standards. *Zubaan* means tongue, voice, language, speech in Hindustani. Zubaan publishes in the areas of the humanities, social sciences, as well as in fiction, general non-fiction, and books for children and young adults under its Young Zubaan imprint.

Typeset in Baskerville 11/14 by Jojy Philip
Printed and bound by Replika Press Pvt. Ltd, India

Contents

CONTENTS

CONTENTS

CONTENTS

Acknowledgements

At the outset I express my sincere gratitude to Zubaan Publishers and Urvashi Butalia for proposing this collection of women's writing from Arunachal Pradesh: it is an important and pioneering initiative and I am honoured to have played a part in its compilation and editing. I am grateful to all the contributors who responded so generously with their writings, all within the first deadline (last summer), when the idea was first mooted. Thank you all for your warm-hearted response and for trusting me with your work. No one could have foreseen that 2020 would turn into a pandemic year with the world in crisis and lockdowns in place across the globe. Everything slowed down with a kind of lockdown also descending on my work with this project.

All I can say now is that it has been a wonderful experience interacting with Zubaan, and with the authors, over telephone and by email, on and off, through the slowness and the isolation, believing that words, thoughts, poetry and prose will always be there to change space and time, offering communication and hope between people even in the darkest and most uncertain of times.

My thanks are also due to Bidisha Mahanta, Sokhep Kri, Moji Riba, Jathi Pulu, friends and colleagues who helped me with a number of contact details so that this volume could be as widely representative of different parts of the state as possible. I also pay my tributes to the Sasakawa Peace Foundation for their enduring commitment and sponsorship.

Introduction

MAMANG DAI

Imagine a group of people huddled around a fire. They are shuddering with cold and hunger. One of them unrolls a piece of rawhide. In the fireglow they see lines and scribbles. The wind is howling outside. Perhaps they are sheltering in a cave. The flames lick at the strange animal skin. It crackles and burns, giving off a delicious aroma. A man with a knife cuts it up into strips. They eat it and continue on their way.

This is a story of a story, one of many to explain the absence of a script among the Arunachal tribes. There is the story of an old man who had the history of his tribe written on deerskin, but this got burnt and he ate it. Another story tells of a deer that lived in the mountains. One day he saw the sons of a legendary ancestor writing the history of the world on a piece of liver. The deer said the men could write on his skin and he would give them back the letters whenever they needed them. In a subsequent hunt the men accidentally killed the deer and ate it.[1]

Of course, this is not to say that the lack of a writing system among the majority of Arunachal tribes was a handicap. Through the years, speech communities continued to thrive with their traditions passed on from generation to generation. The oral tradition has survived with festivals, epic narratives, and the performance of rituals by shamans and rhapsodists who were revered as the guardians of a way of life and custodians of a tribe's collective memory. Indeed much of the northeast region may be dubbed as the land of storytellers.

This book is a first of its kind because it brings together the diverse voices of Arunachal women writing in English and Hindi. There are essays, short fiction, poetry and art. While the state has moved away from the days of the erstwhile NEFA (North-East Frontier Agency) when written records were the work of government departments and anthropologists, today there is an attempt by a growing number of young writers to retrieve oral history with research, collaboration and primary sources as in the works of Mishimbu Miri whose Idu Mishmi legend of 'Athupopu'[2] is included here as a record of the shamanistic faith in a first hand account as the daughter of an Igu, a shaman priest who was renowned for his great powers.

This collection is also enhanced by a good number of young poets, many of whom are working on their first

---

[1] Verrier Elwin. 1958. 'The First Men' in *Myths of the North East Frontier of India.*

[2] Mishimbu Miri. 2018. *Revelations from Idu Mishmi Hymns*, RIWATCH Research Institute of World's Ancient Traditions Cultures and Heritage.

collections, expressing myriad themes of love, longing and remembrance:

> Somewhere, sometime,
> Writing colourful pages
> Filled with the rainbow of happiness
> Then somewhere on blank pages
> Only a cloud of sadness.
> But both the pages belong
> To that open, endless book
> Of unending questions
> Whose answers lie nowhere.

Tunung Tabing: 'Waves of Irony'

While the joys of motherhood, love of the land and questions of the self are evoked in the poems of Doirangsi Kri, Chasoom Bosai, Ponung Ering,[3] Omili Borang, Kolpi Dai, Gyati Ampi and Subi Taba's 'Lost Souls'[4] and the impassioned lyrics of Samy Moyong[5] and Ngurang Reena's poem for her mother are poignant with the anguish of love, they are also fierce with resistance against what it means to be a woman in a traditional society where inherent customary laws dictate how women live their lives, something that often results in untold suffering.

> Before you dismiss me as a mere being
> Someone you could trample and crush and kill
> I just want you to know

---

[3] Ponung Ering. 2014. *Whispers from the Mountains*, New Delhi: Partridge India.

[4] Subi Taba. 2015. *Dear Bohemian Man*.

[5] Samy Moyong. 2019. 'Diigok Rolii' *Solung Souvenir*.

That I was a candle in the woods
Burning bright in an aura of my own

I was a daughter, a sister, a friend, a partner, a wife, a
    mother, a woman, a girl.
I AM – from where you were born.

Samy Moyong: 'I AM'

In 'My Ane's Tribal Love Affair' Ngurang Reena writes:

Ane, I wish I could introduce love to you.
Love is like a rainbow, everyone sees their own,
And the number of colours in yours may vary from
    mine.
But Ane, you can choose your favourite colour.
Ane, I wish you could remarry, and have a friend to
    age with
But our customs prohibit us from tasting love.

They say, *'Donyi-Polo e lenduku'*, ultimately truth
    prevails;
Ane, I will now come home only when the truth
    prevails.
Sorry Ane.
Until then, I will resist for freedom, for you, many
    young girls and me,
Waiting to taste freedom.

There is more poetry originally written in Hindi by
Ayinam Ering, Tolum Chumchum, Tunung Tabing, Nomi
Maga Gumro and Rebom Belo, translated by Gedak Angu,
Yater Nyokir and Takhe Moni. The poems were compiled by
Jamuna Bini, herself a well known poet who also arranged a

meeting of poets so that we could discuss their works for the purpose of this book.

> So what if fate
> decides to leave my roots entangled?
> I'm alive, from inside
> and I've the courage
> to keep growing while confined.
>
> Ayinam Ering: 'I am a Tree'

Jamuna Bini speaks for a generation at the crossroads, faced with the changes transforming our societies while still drawn by the experience of a more innocent time that is rapidly fading, if not already lost forever.

> In this bamboo house
> when the fourteen hearths
> blaze in tune
> the floating flames swim through the bamboo cracks
> and brighten up the world outside
> Now
> We don't live in bamboo houses anymore,
> no more fires burn to glow through the cracks of
>   those bamboo houses.
> Our houses are made of concrete now.
> Our nights are stretched
> sunk in laptops, mobiles and TV,
> SMS, Facebook and WhatsApp have
> become the medium of our bonds.
>
> Jamuna Bini: 'Those Idle Days'

As already mentioned, this is a book of new writings. When someone is asked to contribute poems, an article or any piece of prose, the initial response is that they don't have anything: *I'm not a writer, really, what shall I write about?* I am also guilty of absconding, but once past the blank period I think everyone has something to put down on paper, be it a poetic image, an opinion, a deep conviction or an experience that has stayed with you. It is also paintings and sketches like the ones that illustrate two pages by Bhanu Tatak (a sociology graduate with an interest in art) that provide new ways of seeing and expression.

This collection is a start. The story of writing and what happened to our script may be explained in a story but we know, all over the world, there are numerous endangered languages and many that have vanished forever. The only way to keep such languages alive is to speak the mother tongue. Once upon a time we believed in the 'word' as composed in the epic narratives chanted by the shamans of yore. The shaman was the voice of collective memory, drawing an evolutionary landscape through which the social, ideological and spiritual aspirations of the community were expressed. Added to this there were grandmothers' tales, songs and lullabies. Everyone knew the stories in one form or another and this knowledge linked us together as a group. Today things are different. An issue of fundamental concern is the loss of the mother tongue, especially for those without a writing system as in the languages of Arunachal Pradesh, and this is highlighted in Toko Anu's essay 'Indigenous Tribal Languages of North East India: Strategies for Revitalization', and Yaniam Chukhu's insightful review 'Linguistic Transitions'. While the existing Roman script can be adopted for writing our unwritten languages it is a prerequisite that we have a thorough knowledge of the sounds, vowels and letters of our own languages before we can attempt this transition and this is the problem Arunachal is currently grappling with, since so few today speak or learn their mother tongue in schools or at home.

Another aspect of the preservation of cultural heritage is reflected in Ing Perme's presentation of the *penge*, a dirge that is part of the burial rites of the Adi tribe. This rite is also linked to the shaman tradition. It may appear to be a song of mourning sung by a bereaved family member, or an specially appointed shaman, but if one can sit through the night and understand the archaic language in which a penge is performed, it is a hypnotic journey through a landscape dotted with little anecdotes, place names, streams and fields, in short a conversation towards reconciliation in the face of what is inevitable whereby the departed will travel on in peace and those left behind will find consolation and closure.

In November 2018 Arunachal Pradesh had its first literature festival. The panel discussions ranged from topics such as the origin and development of North East literatures and languages, the pursuit of a script for non-script languages, to exploring the contemporary relevance of oral traditions and manifestations of creativity in folk literature. It would be true to say that in the North East region there are many authors today following the oral tradition to delve into the myths and traditions in a process of retrieval and re-interpretation to inform the writing of today. This is inevitable as it is necessary for literature to grow. The past may be gone, but it is a place we can always re-visit. A tender remembrance is evidence of this in Tongam Rina's tribute to a grandmother who is portrayed as the interpreter of dreams. In a patrilineal society women's names are often lost even though it is women who really are the custodians and transmitters of culture through storytelling, food, clothing, festival preparations, prayer and ritual. The flip side of the coin is the view of women in traditional societies as economic propositions – explored in the photo essay by Karry Padu. This has reference to the customary practice of 'bride price' whereby young women are trapped in marriages transacted by families through the payment of bride price, and tribal traditions that favour men over the rights of women.

In an informative essay entitled 'Bards from the Dawn-lit Mountains' Yater Nyokir outlines the literary scene in the state, tracing the history from the early writers to the present day. In Ronnie Nido's 'The Tina Ceiling' there is a subtle mingling of the aspirations of women covering both sides of the rural-urban divide through a study of the institution of gaon-buras prevalent in the state. There is an ambient air of rites of passage in the prose writing with the 'insider's' attempt to return to one's roots and portray the cultural ethos of a community as in 'Doused Flames' by Leki Thungon and in the subtle, nuanced short story 'The Spectre Dentist' by Millo Ankha. There is disclosure in the recollection of Ponung Ering's 'Among the Voices in the Dark'[6] and Nellie Manpoong's short prose 'Night and I' is a fine example of new writings by women in a succinct, evocative ambience.

Since the state opened up to tourism in the early nineties, Arunachal has been promoted as an unexplored paradise of pristine forests, mountains and rivers. Today Arunachal still

---

[6] Ponung Ering. 2015. *Strewn Petals*. New Delhi: Partridge India.

offers the visitor scenic getaways but the last decades have also seen widescale destruction of forests and environmental damage. Subi Taba's 'The Spirit of the Forest' portrays this sorry state of affairs provoked by the nexus between powerful politicians and vested interests. However, for all our destructive dominance, there is hope that in the end it is Mother Nature who will play her hand and restore equilibrium. Stuti Mamen Lowang echoes this in 'Home is This and Much More', her graphic story of a homeland that is destroyed by the presence of militant groups in a throwback to the days of the timber boom which erupted along with the rise of insurgent activities in the two eastern districts of Tirap and Changlang, the former now bifurcated into Tirap and Longding.

Standing at the crossroads the view is sometimes dimmed by the onslaught of urbanisation and globalisation. This is portrayed in the artwork of Rinchin Choden titled 'Tradition: An Illusion of Continuance'. There are pressing issues at stake, those of culture, identity, environmental degradation and the demise of tradition. Yet, as Rinchin's beautiful drawings testify, there remains 'the silver lining in the dark clouds of modernity', in the drawing captioned 'The Wrap', and this is the central figure of the mother, the hearth and home where we learn who we are.

This book also carries an interview with Tine Mena of Dibang valley district who is the first Arunachal woman and 'everester' from North East India to climb Mount Everest. Tine lives in quiet simplicity and great contentment close to her home district where I caught up with her last winter and met her husband and young son.

At last there is a space for voices calling, and as yet unheard. These voices echo, they question, they are filled with hope. It is my hope, in turn, that these voices will grow, rise, and fill more books and pages with history, culture, stories and poems to make up a unique mosaic of literature that will never be lost in the wider global narrative. In the words of Toni Morrison,

> You are your own stories and therefore free to imagine and experience what it means to be human without wealth. What it feels like to be human without domination over others, without reckless arrogance, without fear of others unlike you, without rotating, rehearsing and reinventing the hatreds you learned in the sandbox. And although you don't have complete control over the narrative (no author does, I can tell you), you could nevertheless create it.[7]

So here it is. I hope the reader will enjoy this book. If we ate the words and lost our script I say let's set the words free.

Mamang Dai
Itanagar, Arunachal Pradesh
August 2020

---

[7] Tony Morrison. 2014. Commencement address at Wellesley College.

A Man I Know

SAMY MOYONG

He writes on rainy and windy days
of a woman mysterious and fierce
He writes on grey and gloomy days
of life and its lessons learnt
He writes about the moon and the evening skies
of sunrises and sunsets
He writes about the breeze and the cold
and the loneliness of his heart
He writes about love and leaving
of words unsaid but felt
He writes about smiles and elegance
of the scarred heart and lowly souls
He writes about dreams and longings
of fireworks and blooming flowers
He sounds like a man with a soul, restless,
to which only a poet can relate
He writes with his heart
but laughs it off

calls it musings and scribbles
He puts on a mask when asked of his day
and talks of everything but himself
He calls himself evil but acts like a human
confusing himself and all others
He writes of the clouds and their drift
and seems obsessed,
He seems like a man with deep desires
living in his yesteryears
I might be wrong with all my words
never been good at reading people,
but of this I know I am not wrong
that he writes on rainy and windy days
both of his heart and the world outside
He writes on rainy and windy days
and on grey and gloomy days.

From: *Echoes of the Heart*

I AM

SAMY MOYONG

Before you dismiss me as a mere being
Someone you could trample and crush and kill
I just want you to know

That I was a candle in the woods
Burning bright in an aura of my own
I was a sparkling drop of water
In the land of the parched
I was the golden light
When the sun rose in the east
The evening glow before the night set in
I was the twinkle of the stars
The shine of the moon
The warmth of the sun
The cool of rain
Laughter, comfort and everything good

I was a daughter, a sister, a friend, a partner, a wife, a
    mother, a woman, a girl.
I AM – from where you were born.

I had dreams like everyone had
I wanted to be someone, like everyone wants
I breathed air, I felt emotions
I walked, I talked, I ran and I sang

I was quite like you
Without a fear in the world
I was quite like you
Hopeful and full of dreams
I was quite like you
Ambitious and courageous,
Before you decided to take me away
Bundle me up and gobble me up
To satisfy that monstrous hunger of yours
Tear me up and kill my soul

Didn't your heart wince a little?
Didn't your hands tremble a little?
Didn't your conscience question a little?
Didn't your mind think again a little?
And in that moment of your act
I saw you die more than me
I saw a beast weaker than me
I saw someone lost in the woods
I saw you and I saw loathing
I saw you and I saw dirt
I saw you and I saw emptiness

Each time you raised your fingers up the length of my
    skirt
The depth of my cleavage
And the time of the night I return home
Each time you raised your fingers on the gender of
    my friends
My character and my behaviour

But now
I ask,
Do even diapers turn you on?

Men
You puny, little men.
Don't call yourself that
For you are far from being a man
And so now
All that I have got left to say is
When all you can think of is about the pleasure
Of that extended flesh hanging between your thighs

I wish the vagina could bite.

First published: *Diigok Roli, Solung souvenir, 2019.*

Revelations from Idu Mishmi Hymns

MISHIMBU MIRI

My belief in shamanism and its various practices is very
deep because I have been witness to the faith healing of
the Idu Mishmi shamans – Igus – since my childhood,
and I have gone through the experience of being healed
myself. As the daughter of an Idu Mishmi shaman, I was
privileged to interact with a number of divine shamans of
my community. My late father, Rano Miri, wanted me to
become a great, powerful shaman like him. He encouraged
me to listen to his hymns, chant them carefully, and follow
his words. He let me participate in the shamanic rituals
and taught me how to play different ritualistic instruments.
He also took me to various ceremonies to explain the
importance and meaning of hymns. It was his idea to write
down the revelations of the sacred hymns and what follows
is one such narrative as explained to me by my father and
noted down by me.

Athupopu

Athupopu is a sacred place for the Idu Mishmi community and its existence finds mention in the sacred hymns. It is located near Keya pass and is considered a holy pilgrimage for the Idus. The rock at Athupopu still bears the palm impression of the great Igu Sinewru. The place around the rock is completely dry but the rock itself oozes water; according to the sacred hymns this water represents the tears of Sinewru.

Sinewru, the great Igu, once went to the land of the Far East called Etoti-Iyreti to perform the ritual ceremony of death called Yaah. Before he left his home he put a spell on his house and his family to protect them so that he could travel far and wide and perform rituals without worrying about them.

One day, on his return journey, he stopped at Athupopu to rest. As he rested, Anzome Ishuwru, the fulvous-breasted woodpecker came to him and said, 'A small grave has been dug in the compound behind your house!' Sinewru laughed aloud. 'Don't be a pretentious well-wisher greedy to have a share of my Igu Gruwu [the gifts given to the Igu in return for ritual performances]. Before leaving the house I had cast a spell on my house so that no evil would dare enter.'

'I swear by the gods that I haven't come with any greed,' said Ishuwru, 'The truth is someone has died in your home. If you don't believe me, why don't you try finding out for yourself from the path of the dead by your ayuwu taa,[1] made

---

[1] Ayuwu taa is a stick made of bunches of leaves with a 'v' shape at the end (fishtail palm) used by the priest in death rituals to guide the soul of the dead.

of the leaves that were born with Sinewru?' Sinewru thought for a while, and then he kept his ayuwu taa with some signs on the path that was used by the souls of the dead to travel to the next world. After a while he found that a soul had passed by and it was the soul of his mother. Sinewru burst into tears as he sat on the rock of Popu with one palm resting on the other rock. He wept as he said that there was an alternative for everything on earth except for a mother. Sinewru's tears are still found rolling down from the rock at Popu and an impression of his palm is still visible on the rock face.

At his home his dead mother returned to the house and requested her daughter-in-law to clean her by removing all the worms that had grown in her body. But the daughter-in-law was frightened by her appearance and drove her away using her weaving stick. The mother had nowhere to go. She wandered around in the forest. An owl followed her; it had watched her being driven out of the house. The owl said, 'Come with me. I shall remove all the worms and insects from your body and make you look good and beautiful again.' But the owl took the mother down into the valley and devoured her.

In the meanwhile Sinewru reached home and now decided to perform the ritual ceremony for the salvation of his mother's soul, but the body of his mother was nowhere to be found. Sinewru also came to know of the ill treatment given to his mother by his wife.

Anzuwru[2] was invoked to find out the truth. Anzuwru then made the prophecy that the owl had eaten her. When

---

[2] Anzuwru is the god of prophecy who does not have any physical form but is a voice one hears.

questioned, the owl denied this. Anzuwru then said to the owl in front of everyone, 'No, you cannot deny this. The ball of hair of the dead person is still stuck in your throat. The smell of the corpse is coming from your mouth and I can see the soul of the mother wandering around in your beak.'

Then the owl at last accepted the guilt of eating Sinewru's mother. Sinewru then called back the soul of his mother from the mouth of the owl. After this her soul was fed at the doorstep and was told that this was its last meal at home. This is called Athrowoyatha. From that moment on she would have to start her journey to the eternal world with all her belongings and her share of wealth. Sinewru also told her that he would lead her to the place of origin of her ancestors before leading her to the eternal world forever. After this journey his mother would live a satisfactory afterlife and would never return to the world of the living. Sinewru performed the five-day ritual ceremony called Yaah and gave salvation to his mother forever. It is believed that this moment marks the beginning of the performance of the death ceremony, Yaah, that continues to this day.

I Am a Tree

AYINAM ERING

I am a tree
I'm strong. I'm steady.
So what if autumn turns my leaves yellow?
So what if the assailant wind strips all my
branches bare?
I'm still alive, from inside,
and I possess the strength
to spread greenery again.

I am a tree
I'm strong. I'm steady.
So what if the rain
Drenches me to the core?
So what if the sun
scorches me?
I'm still alive, from inside
and pass this gift
to deal with adversity with pride.

I am a tree.
I'm soft. I'm gentle.
So what if I'm left defeated
by the passing seasons?
So what if fate
decides to leave my roots entangled?
I'm alive, from inside
and I have the courage
to keep growing while confined.

Offspring

AYINAM ERING

First born was a girl
A blissful air of rejoicing in the house
filled with relatives
Sumptuous array of food served
adorning the child with endless names
Waving goodbye
Blessing – the next born to be a boy.

But the next born was a girl too.
A smaller amount of food served
Not as many names suggested
Yet again,
A third girl child.
Whoever came this time
Blessed, but with a regretful sigh.

Fourth, A girl again.
A worry seemed to descend

On the faces
Fearful for the father's lineage.

Fifth. A girl once more!
Ah!
A second marriage was suggested
By the well wishers.
When the sixth was a girl as well
No one came.
A gloomy silence benumbed their hearts
Only the wails of the labouring mother
filled the room
Joined by silent howls
Of the daughters in the corner,
And the new born
covered in blood
cried clueless, on the mother's lap.

Tradition
An Illusion of Continuance

RINCHIN CHODEN

Tradition is dying. No matter how hard we try to cling on
to our mythical past, the world will, sooner or later, swallow
us whole. This is the basis for 'An Illusion of Continuance'.
The feeling that we are running in circles, trying to rekindle
a lost flame that has almost been put out by the ever-
encroaching hands of urbanisation and globalisation. Our
efforts all but remain an illusion.

Bait and Switch

The crusade against plastic has been ongoing for generations. Although the end result is well worth the effort, we cannot help but feel as though the battle is already lost, for we are growing ever more dependent on plastic as the years go by.

The Airy Fury

There is a wooden mask that is used by monks for traditional dances; this is one way in which many cultures pay tribute to nature and all it provides. However, the manner in which we treat the environment today will lead us to a sombre inevitability: that wooden mask will soon be replaced by a gas mask.

The Identity

Different cultures have always had different standards of beauty. While there was a time when these standards were praised for their uniqueness and tribes were celebrated for their individuality, the growing popularity of Western beauty standards is sweeping over the world, and 'generic' is the new norm.

The Jigsaw Puzzle

There are certain tribes in our state that even we, as Arunachalis, don't
know of. Ironically, we laugh hysterically at videos of people who do not
know about North East India, when we barely know about it ourselves.
We need to put the pieces of our own puzzles together before we go
about blaming 'outsiders'.

The Wrap

The silver lining in the dark clouds of modernity. The mother; the home
and the solace where we first learn about tradition. We need to respect
her and learn from her about the outside world. Her warm embrace
teaches us to not falter in the face of adversity.

Night and I

NELLIE N. MANPOONG

I arrive home, turn the key in the heavy lock and switch on the lights to an empty room. Take my phone out from my daypack and fidget with it for a while. Check whether I have any messages or not. Empty notifications don't exactly have me jumping with joy, so I lay that curse-of-a-phone down on the table by the side.

I walk past the lounge chairs and into the bedroom. Change into whatever makes me comfortable and head back into the living room.

I pick up the phone again; I thought I felt it vibrate. A few messages that don't really concern me.

I throw my favourite red quilt on the couch before I head towards the kitchen where the alcohol lies hiding. Know that it is not hiding from anyone but me. I pick up a coffee mug, not a crystal glass, and pour what I presume is 60 ml in clubs.

I take a sip of that smooth, disgusting whiskey – smooth because it is expensive, disgusting because it burns my throat when I take a pretentious sip. A few chunks of ice and you are set for still nights.

I head back to the living room, pull up my quilt and get comfortable on the cotton-filled mattress, surrounded on three sides by patio-sized couches and the television mounted on the fourth. It often feels like a fortress.

My neighbour's dogs start to bark and I know he is approaching.

There is an abrupt, gentle knock at the door and I force myself out of my self-proclaimed den.

He is cold, always dressed in darkness, and mostly silent – he loves the silence.

He turns towards the switchboard and dims the lights like always; he says the light hurts his eyes.

I turn on the television and switch to a channel playing music; the music helps kill the silence we often sit through. I look at him from the corner of my eyes, conjuring up such thoughts: I am not him; I wouldn't want to be him. Why does his stillness have a piercing effect on me?

As my mind plays some thinking games, he disappears into the kitchen and returns with a glass filled with whiskey – same old 60 ml.

I've often had conversations which didn't make sense at ungodly hours, but night has come down like he always does and I don't want to be rude, so we have our once-in-a-lonely-moon conversation; not in words, but in motions-emotions.

He calls for another round of whiskey; I oblige. He brings the now half empty 750 ml bottle for a few more rounds and I agree. The wall clock placed on the bookshelf seems to tick away faster than usual and night begins to look a little sombre, a little empty.

I hold onto him: I feel him shiver, his eyes, like a black onyx stone start to well up, and the silence breaks into a sob. He wraps his arms around me and his emotions cruise into my veins like a lethal shot of cocaine. We lie down, together-alone, exhausted and shut our minds to the world outside.

Time speeds by and dawn breaks. I see a note by my side: 'I shall return when darkness descends.'

Dying Lights

PONUNG ERING ANGU

Darkness clouds over the streaming lights
As the distance seems to grow
We linger in the mists
A fairytale love no more

We'll find a way out of the dark
Like the star that lights up the path
As the horizon draws in closer to us
Our souls will rise from the ashes and the dust

We shall look ahead as we were taught when young
Never lose our faith and our love
The will that keeps us going
And the love that strengthens our soul

As the dawn breaks over and the darkness dies
Things are easy but nothing ever lasts
Oh the love, the strength and our enduring will
Are stuck somewhere in the walls of a past.

The Tina Ceiling

RONNIE NIDO

'Have you ever heard of this thing called feminism?' I asked.

'What is that?' Yarup responds, raising her eyebrows a little.

'Well, it is the movement which believes that men and women are equal in every way.'

'But aren't we already equal?'

'Yes, we are. But sometimes we are not treated equally you know, like how no woman has ever become Head Gaon Bura.'

'So, you are telling me that in our next meeting I can assert that women and men are equal these days, so make women Head Gaon Buras too.'

'Absolutely.'

'Then I am definitely going to say that. Maybe you should come to the next meeting.'

'Yes, it will be like a date.'

'What is a date?' Yarup's eyebrows rise again.

This snippet of conversation is reflective of Yarup's campaign to become a Head Gaon Buri of her village. As the Secretary of the All Kamle District Gaon Bura and Gaon Buri Association (AKDGBGBA), Yarup has proven her competence time and again. Their Association is crucial to the appointment of new Gaon Buras in the region. The due process of making such an appointment is a public meeting of the association on the selected list, which is documented as official minutes, and then signed by each attendee. The signed document is then dispatched to the office of the Deputy Commissioner of the respective district, who remains the final approving authority.

Gaon Buras and Gaon Buris – the terms literally translate as Village (elder) men and Village (elder) women, who are identified in the community by their bright red coats. A mark of authority, knowledge and wisdom, these red coats were given to the elders of the village. These elders are part of the local governance system in the form of village councils, in all their various forms. These councils are present across the tribes of Arunachal Pradesh with varied names. Some tribes follow the hereditary rule, with the power transferring from father to son. But among the Nyishis of Kamle district (formerly the Hill Miri subtribe) in Arunachal Pradesh the position was based on nomination. While the criteria for such nominations are not codified, prior research points to age, experience, knowledge of the traditional laws with a sound judgement and wealth status as important factors in the nomination. However, little has been discussed about who appoints these elders. A strong feature, from listening to the stories in the public domain, is that most of these elders were male. The existing literature categorically mentions, 'No sex distinction is made though there is quite less (sic) participation from the females.'

But things changed in the early 1990s with transformations in the political atmosphere of the state and the social dynamics within the Hill Miri community, as the historically isolated community started assimilating with the formal institutions of democracy. There were mass campaigns against child marriage and a campaign for women's empowerment. So the community felt the need to bring women into the local governance structure. And thus, in Kamle district eight women were nominated and given the red coats and consequently named as Gaon Buris.

About twelve to thirteen Gaon Buras/Buris are appointed every year but these nominations are not without political gains. In the ossature of self-governance and representative governance, the latter has taken the upper hand by yielding their powers towards the appointment of the former.

What began as public leaders seeking out generous, fair and *chokob* (smart) personalities have now evolved into our own form of barter – votes for the position of Gaon Bura/ Buri. In a constituency where the direction of its voters is based on kinship ties and affinity, the power move deployed over and again is to give a job to the head of a large family in order to secure his family's vote. Usually these heads of families are elderly men, so a natural consequence is to appoint them as Gaon Buras.

However, such politically motivated nominations come with their own constraints. Even at the average rate of ten Gaon Buras per year, it would result in thousands of Gaon Buras, a number unsustainable by the administration and present day funding systems. A solution has thus been found in funding these appointments under the MLALAD (Members of Legislative Assembly Land Area Development) fund.

But a characteristic about MLAs and other public leaders remains that they change every five years. Thus an MLA voted out ends up leaving behind a row of powerless and temporary Gaon Buras, and even Gaon Buris (in some instances). As the effect of being on the losing side hits very close to home, the people then go to extreme lengths to ensure that their candidates win.

'Every election season it is impossible to go outside as there are fights after fights. We have stopped interfering because the fights won't stop unless the election is over and the winning party has been declared. It starts from the Panchayat election and then goes up till the general elections. The Panchayat leaders are more powerful than us and we are asked not to interfere in their business,' Yarup said.

In a strange turn of events, in May of 2018, the five-year term of the last PRI (Panchayati Raj Institutions) members expired and the government has delayed the re-election process despite judicial intervention. In this atmosphere of missing public leaders, the Gaon Bura(s)/Buri(s) find themselves with an unprecedented surge in their powers. Further, adding to their weight is the loss of trust in their leaders by the public. The Trans-Arunachal Highway which was supposed to connect their villages and bring prosperity is caught in a web of corruption. And the public are waking up to the price they have to pay for this blatant abuse of power.

It is in this context that the Gaon Buras/Buris have been given a new charter of duties in the past few months: verification of the Trans-Arunachal highway compensation schemes, verification of the Inner Line Permit and verification of Schedule Tribe – Permanent Resident Certificate, along with their previous duties of maintaining peace. They are in a position to investigate, report and punish, all at the same time.

'People may think it looks great but it is not so. We received a one-time annual honorarium. Our condition gets worse afterwards. The government says we are not supposed to be involved in politics and yet they call us for every kind of political work. The resources are given to us only as an afterthought. Instead, people often accuse us of corruption too as they say we reap political benefits that we don't share with them,' says Yarup.

Such accusations exist because, more often than not, Gaon Buras give favourable judgements to members of their own kin. Further, a head Gaon Bura can quash the collective judgements of other Gaon Buras without explanation which, if unfair, paints all of them in a negative light. 'We know that the losing party, in any case, will never be happy. So, we take the criticisms in our stride,' says Yarup. Luckily, for the community there exists no contempt of court.

Further, existing with a formal judicial system has contributed towards the Gaon Buras with their emblematic red coats losing their original standing. A strict order from the government requires them to submit all non-cognizable offences to the magistrate's court. Contradicting such orders leads to the authorities pulling out the big guns. And a coat is no match for guns, regardless of the colour.

Everything said though, being in a leadership position as the woman secretary makes Yarup confident about her own competence to be a Head Gaon Buri. The process only requires her to submit a letter of intention to the office of the Deputy Commissioner and her candidature being supported by two other Gaon Buras of the village. And Yarup knows the two people she will be counting on to support her candidature.

Yarup, like most women of her generation, was betrothed, in effect sold, when she was a toddler, but she ran away when she grew up and fell in love with her husband. A fact she regrets because 'I gave my parents so much pain. They had to pay double the mithuns as I never went back.' She has come a long way since, in claiming what she is owed.

After we discuss her plans to be Head Gaon Buri and all the things she would establish on becoming a head Gaon Buri, like letting women have the choice to break marriages that were fixed in their infancy, reducing the fine incurred on breaking child marriages and letting women speak in the trials alongside their husbands and fathers, I tell her to 'go break the glass ceiling'.

She asks me what it means.

I tell her and she responds, 'Only the rich would make ceilings out of glass. I am very content with the tina ceiling that I have.'

'But won't it be tougher to break the tina ceiling? Glass is easier to break, you know.'

'No. A few hits at the right places and the nails which hold it, the tina comes off. Glass is expensive and gives a sense of loss when it breaks but tina, even a torn one, can be used again and again as fence in our fields, as trays for feeding the pigs, as a roof for the chicken coop and even to divert drains at times.'

'And because of its value in repurposing, it will be easier to break it?' I ask.

'Yes. Broken glass, even the expensive kind, doesn't have much use around here.'

I make a mental resolution to keep my vacillating urban metaphorical concepts to myself.

Home is This and Much More

STUTI MAMEN LOWANG

The Wooden House

GYATI T. M. AMPI

Rustling leaves,
Creaking doors,
And the rustic feel.

Familiar footsteps,
Hushed voices,
And the warmth of fire.

Fragrance, oh! So sweet,
Whispered old tales,
And lingering souls lit.

Walked up the gravel path,
Smiled just like the old times,
And the house became home again.

My Ane's Tribal Love Affair

NGURANG REENA

When love has to breast the dead
What does mother know of love, I wonder!

Ever since her husband's death, she has been cursing
    her God Donyi Polo;
Ane Donyi – Mother Sun, and Abu Polo – Father
    Moon,
Nga nyulune hiye mingpa? Who killed my husband?
Bute Nyibu – priest, the mediator between the spirits
    and humans
The most competent of all, was called to negotiate
    with the spirits of the forest.
In her quest to seek answers for his death many *Sibe,*
    Irik, Puru were sacrificed
Mithun, pigs and chicken
The *nyedar-namlo* altar covered in blood and animal
    carcasses;
My Ane's impersonal powers.

The *Nyibus* are believed to possess a tongue that
    communicates beyond earth
Performing rituals and carrying messages to the spirits.
But seven hundred and thirty days later the spirits
    remain reticent.
My Ane is breeding pigs in her backyard; perhaps the
    shaman will be summoned back soon!

It was an unfamiliar time when traditional faith
    entwined with western ideas:
'I will offer my healthiest pig to Donyi Polo when I
    find who the killer is,' she said.
While her husband lay six feet under with candles
    and a bible beside him,
Nyisang Nyubu and the church priest together blessed
    her husband.

Ever since her husband's death she has been cursing
    her God Donyi Polo.
Ever since her husband's death, my Ane has forgotten
    to appreciate the *Nyokum Yullo* festival
    My Ane's Tribal Love Affair !
At thirteen, 'traded' for a few mithun to my father
At thirteen, ready-made for a pact, oh heavenly father

While Ane's friends Yalam and Yapi wrapped
    themselves in school uniforms,
Ane trapped herself in the inevitable transaction, a
    sacred contract
Blessed by the spirits of the forest, her forefathers, her
    ancient tradition.

Two of her sisters Nyaku and Yami had the same fate,
Sold to older men in the village.
The inescapable transaction; a sacred contract.
Blessed by spirits of the forest, their forefathers, their
    ancient tradition.

Many moons and suns later, there was another
    woman; my father had remarried.
'I am sorry,' said my father.
'It was the right thing to do,' said my forefathers, my
    brothers and my neighbours.

My Ane was just the 'first wife' now
What does mother know of love, I wonder!
A betrayal in the transaction, a betrayal in tradition
What does mother know of love, I wonder!

Illiterate and frail,
Left to sour
Like a fermented bean,
Left to procreate.

Life has not been a bed of roses for her.
She slept on the thorns, alone.
But mothers never leave!
An umbilical cord never severs
Their imprint on their children is stronger than the
    belief in gods.

She was young once,
But now the world is decrepit

And all good things have come to an end.
When love has to breast the dead,
Love dies, like dry wells of tears.

As I write, I am thinking of my Ane's face,
She is sitting by the Immi-fireplace, draped in finely
    crafted wrinkles,
Aged legs clothed in the old *Gale* wrapping her
    stricken heart.

She must be making fodder for her *Eriks*, she has nine
    of them!
Her face against the burning flame in our Nyasang
    Naam-Bamboo house
Reminds me of my father's dead body
Like waves of creases after many hours of drowning.
She moves the firewood and the smoke sighs in
    acceptance,
Ah, I can now count the wrinkles on her face
    precisely.
One two and three and I, consigned to oblivion,
Her wrinkles remind me of time.

Ane,
You have lost time,
Innocence, childhood, womanhood.
Ane, you have lost all.
Your story was devoid of love;
Like a song without a melody, discordant all along,
But you kept singing the tune, and you still have the
    song on your lips.

When you love someone more than your life, you
    suffer.
And in time, you may learn not to miss him.
But you will always carry Abu with you;
He is alive in you and the changing seasons.

Ane, I wish I could introduce love to you.
Love is like a rainbow, everyone sees their own,
And the number of colours in yours may vary from
    mine.
But Ane, you can choose your favourite colour.
Ane, I wish you could remarry, and have a friend to
    age with
But our customs prohibit us from tasting love.

And Ane,
We are two different clocks made in two different times,
Old and new, an oxymoron.
We are two different women of two different times,
In your old tradition and my evolution, an antithesis.
It's a man's world Ane, and I must resist,
For you, many young girls and I are waiting to taste
    freedom.

And Ane,
Ever since Abu's death, I have been cursing my God
    too!
Donyi Polo, Ane Donyi,
Nga Abuni hiye mingpa? Who killed my father?

My breath reeks of my dead father and the betrayal.
His *Bopa, Letum,* his *Dao* – stench of my clan, my tribe,
Headgear, men's traditional cloth, machette.
Treachery and dishonesty are all I can sense.
Where is the kinship? Where is the brotherhood, Ane?

Undeterred by violence, fettered by the hurt
I am a wounded dove, I have forgotten what peace
    smells like.
Yet I will carry folklore, magic, the spirits of *Nyapin*
    with me.
I will revere my prayers and my traditions.
I am carrying my tribe on my back,
knowing that we will always be one in this today,
    tomorrow, and in death.

'Truth is the soul and resolve of Donyi-Polo,' my Abu
    told me once.
Then where is the truth, Ane?
I have scoured heaven and earth for answers.
They say, *'Donyi-Polo e lenduku'* – ultimately truth
    prevails;
Ane, I will now come home only when the truth
    prevails.
Sorry, Ane.
Until then, I will resist for freedom for you, many
    young girls and me,
Waiting to taste freedom.

Which Part of Me

KOLPI DAI

I don't know which part of me is real
The one that hides in the room,
Or the one that dares to face the crowd.

The tears I shed in pain, or
The laughter I spread.
The household girl that stays in,
Or the lady that walks out in pride.
The little girl afraid to confront,
Or the strong headed girl embarking out.
The girl that shies away,
Or the girl who works things out.

Sometimes, I am a sunflower,
and sometimes a rose.

The Interpreter of Dreams

TONGAM RINA

This is about Nyikam, an old woman and my grandmother, my first teacher who spoke no Hindi, English or Assamese.

The trusted weather-woman, brilliant interpreter of dreams, laugh riot, bad cook and a lousy storyteller. But a heart as deep as the sea and as vast as the sky and as serene as the summer breeze in the hills.

She, who taught me to forage wild leaves and mushrooms and fish using a wild herb, collect wild yam and to dig deep for it. She helped me cross the swinging cane and bamboo bridge on a sunny, slippery morning. Sometimes she just left me halfway, screaming, as I tried to balance while she half danced, laughing nonstop and rocked the bridge.

She, who was the interpreter of dreams, who knew who was dying and whether there was going to be an epidemic.

She, who made me write letters. Most of the time addresses were misplaced and the letters never sent.

She, who taught me that people age and that walking is an ordeal, going to the bathroom is much harder and farting comes easy. And that there is no shame in peeing in your clothes. It's all about age and there is no point fighting time and the ailments it brings along.

My first feminist, who believed in a world that's equal and fair for all.

Someone who taught me to keep a secret and value unspoken, unwritten codes of lifelong friendships with humans, animals, plants based on pure trust and sharing.

She, who taught me to feed salt to the mithuns and that cats and dogs can be friends. And if they are not, leave them alone. Some things, you can't force or change.

The teacher of life skills – chopping wood, making rice in the bamboo tube, carrying wood in a cane and bamboo basket, winnowing, preparing the local brew, roasting meat, fish and chillies to perfection.

The one who taught me to sing songs while harvesting, rituals, swimming in the cold white river, interpreting the songs of birds and the howls of foxes.

She, who knew which year the oranges and pineapples, would be sweet. One look at the sky, and she knew how the weather was going to pan out. She could see the rain from a thousand miles, through the thick dark mountain.

Looking back, I regret not being a good enough student.

The lifelong comforter knew her end was coming two months beforehand, as she refused treatment and took refuge in prayers and waiting. The only thing that she used was a balm prescribed by her doctor grandchild to ease her body pain.

I met her last in her favorite bamboo and wood kitchen surrounded by her grandchildren and great-grandchildren. As we parted, she held my hands and said it was our last meeting and that I should not cry.

A few weeks later, I sat and watched as she lay still, not to wake up again, and someone broke into a song, a lamentation celebrating her life, sung with the pain, longing and finality of everything that is mortal.

Perhaps with time, memories and the pain and longing that come along with it will wane. I am yet to say my final goodbye or even acknowledge that she has left forever. I wonder if she still roasts potatoes and whether she met grandfather.

And suddenly, it's four years now that she has been gone. Four years when I have missed her, when I have dreamed and wondered how she would have interpreted my dreams, and when I have yearned to share another glass of poka with her. But I know that is not to be. I know I have to learn to cherish her memories and remember her in my heart.

And even today, when I go back home to the familiar hearth at the centre of the house, where relatives chat, share a drink and talk about life, I cannot get myself to accept the roasted potatoes that they offer me. Some memories are too intimate to get used to.

From the Jungle Series

BHANU TATAK

Scribbled Pages

KOLPI DAI

Somebody told me the love in paper is wrong.
The stories in paper are wrong.
Because I only know to speak in paper
I shut my mouth and let them whisper.

I would stare at the windows,
wondering and fantasizing as the wind blew,
scribbling on the pages with ink –
mixture of feelings, doubts and findings,

But one day I threw all of it in rage,
silence, fear and pain were all its wage.
Alas!
Looking for the scribbled pages
for innocence, love and faith,
the price for growing decent –
with the papers left blank and unscribbled.

Doused Flames

LEKI THUNGON

'O Aano Norbu! Ahang ne?' Oh, Anu Norbu, are you well?

Aka Rinchin's voice tore through the hum of a bright summer day. Norbu turned her head left and then right to locate the source of this greeting. 'Anu! Here!' The voice resounded ahead of her. She squinted and capped her hand over her eyes and saw a lanky man with a sparse moustache. It was her paternal grandfather's nephew, her uncle. She made a quick genealogical calculation based on the last discussion with her father. While drawing a complicated family chart, her father had revealed the patrilineal logic behind the history of her community; family history could be furthered only through men. The female members of the family were only temporary members in the kinship map of the clan. Norbu believed that this was an incomplete family tree because it left the mothers and daughters hanging like the vestigial wings of an extinct bird. She left these thoughts to ferment in her subconscious for posterity.

Whenever summer holidays approached, her good-humoured father would transform into an irritable and quick-tempered patriarch. Perhaps around those times he realised that his life choice to marry an outsider had indeed affected the future of his progeny back home. To avoid further reproach from his brothers who stayed behind, he would prepare his children for the annual visit to his village. Every summer before the vacation he would prepare a presentation on genealogy and family history. At the end of each class the trio, Norbu, her father and her brother, Lakpa would have used up pages of notebooks with flow charts and Tibetan names written hurriedly in Roman script. By the second summer this practice was established as an integral part of the family vacation package. Norbu, unlike her brother, earnestly ingested all the information about her paternal lineage. She was especially intrigued by the rules of matrimony which determined people's designations and ritualistic position in the kinship line. It became a game for her; she would often compete with her younger brother on guessing the kinship terminology of distant relatives. Who would be called (in relation and not necessarily by blood) 'Aka' as opposed to 'Azang'. But when she learnt about how she and her mother were only branches in the family tree that connected different clans and communities, she felt betrayed. Her father found her concern valid but needless for the time being. The query had to wait another ten years at least, the present scenario called for her to only focus on getting the genealogical designations right. The thought had fermented since.

The lanky man with a thin moustache should be called 'Aka' and not 'Azang', she resolved.

She cleared her throat, gulped a generous amount of air into her lungs and shouted back, 'Ahang, Aka! Nang ahang ne?' I am good, what about you? As these familiar but foreign words rolled out of her tongue, she could hear her voice scraping the roof of her mouth and stretching the limits of her lungs. A casual conjecture amongst the Sherdukpens was that people who live on the banks of an agile river develop a higher decibel level out of sheer necessity. How else would they have called out to their friends and family from across the river? This speculation continues to live amongst the generation of smart phones and internet for its comic element. The river too remains agile.

'Mu amba?' What? Aka Rinchin replies loudly, with ease.

Norbu couldn't help but appreciate how her uncle's voice, unlike hers, did not lose its tone with distance. She lived amongst concrete buildings, asphalt streets and tarred roads. Her voice did not cut it.

She ran towards her uncle's patio and repeated that she was doing well and inquired about his health and well-being, all in a single question, 'Nang ahang ne?'

'Ahang ba! Ado Ramba?' When did you come?

Shit. He didn't use a single recognizable key word. Words like 'Delhi', 'Ama', 'Achi', 'Anu Khao', 'school' often slipped meanings into sentences in the language she never learnt. She scanned her limited Sherdukpen vocabulary to no respite. She switched to Hindi, a language everyone in Sethu understood. 'Parents are fine too,' she murmured.

'I meant when did you come? See, you must come more often to your village; ask your father to teach you your language.' He added gently as if to apologise for discouraging the child, 'It's good to know your own language, no?'

'Yes.' She smiled the most the genuine smile. Her eyes arched into a half moon.

'You want some *kakung* and *hung ja*?'

She nodded enthusiastically. If getting out of this sticky situation meant having another snack and a tasty one at that, why not?

Her uncle put aside the axe on the freshly chopped pile of wood. The sun dried pieces were already stacked neatly at the end of the marbled patio. Both his sons, Pema Tsering and Pema Khandu, were civil engineers working with the Public Works Department. The young men had done well for themselves and thus held a respectable status in the village. Their social ranking and their material success were not necessarily incidental. To provide for one's parents and family is considered to be one of the primary duties of a good man. They were good men, very good men. When she stepped on the patio, she was startled to find her aunt, Atung Yeshi, crouched next to Aka chopping fresh *tamul* with a nut cracker. The concrete railing had completely concealed the stocky woman.

'Oh Anu, you came.' She smiled; this was not a question in Sethu; this was yet another form of greeting and acknowledgment.

'Lets go to the kitchen?' her Aka suggested.

The kitchen stood two feet away from the main house. While most houses in her village had transformed from stone and wood to cement and glass, everyone preferred to have a traditional wooden kitchen with a hearth in the middle. She followed the couple through the front door; they crossed the living room meant for official purposes: this was the place where high ranking officers were entertained with local drinks and food. It was important to give guests a glimpse into the village's tradition of hospitality. If these events went well, a relationship of mutual respect and boundary would be established by the end of it. This was also the place where relatively well-off and socially higher families would receive Rimboches to perform rituals of purification and other imperatives to maintain a balance between the subtle world and a growing world of materiality. Norbu visited these memories she was never part of in reality, scenes of all the hearty events in this room where men were spokespersons, women were happy complements, and children were pushed into a room or two with enough snacks to forget about the adults. Her eyes suddenly fell on the beautiful white crocheted table cloth. The TV too was covered as if in modesty with a bright pink crochet cloth. So were the little side tables covered in yellow. This overindulgence with crochet ended with the living room. Her aunty caught her staring at the creations.

'Our youngest Anu made this! She has a knack for household chores. Now that she is gone to finish her B.Com in Bomdila, there is no one to decorate the house.'

They asked her about her school, the lessons she was learning, what she wanted to be.

'A doctor,' she replied without thinking. It always made everyone happy. She could never understand the language of math and had no idea what she really wanted to be as an adult. She knew for now that she just wanted to run to the river and try and climb trees with her cousins. Even farm, if her mother allowed her this summer. Her mother would miss no opportunity to remind her of the value of an untanned complexion.

Meanwhile, her aunt rekindled the fire in the *bukhari* and reheated the water in the pot which Norbu knew for a fact was never left empty on the hearth. An empty vessel on a hearth brought bad luck; the water-filled pot was the household amulet for every respectable family in Sethu. She got the butter from the wooden cabinet. A row of aluminium and brass ladles hanging at its side glinted like the silver and golden keys of a piano. The wooden kitchen with the burning hearth is the heart of a household's life in this part of the land. Family meals, familial truces, neighbourly visits and discussions on political affairs and scandals often unfolded around the warmth of the hearth. The state of this private and social space allegedly reflects the state of the household. A clean and organized kitchen, lined with shiny utensils, signified a good household order. Good wife, good daughters, good sons and a father who hasn't lost his authority.

A plate of cream-filled biscuits appeared in front of Norbu with the kakung. Her aunt brought them from the modern kitchen inside the house. She placed the same treats before her husband before helping herself to them. They ate in relative silence interspersed with Norbu's inconsequential questions about their kitchen garden. She picked up her pace and finished the remaining buttery liquid in three gulps to quickly relieve herself from the awkward hospitable situation, but just then her cousin burst in. He was Aka Rinchin's cousin's son who had married Atung Yeshi's younger sister. He would be an Abu, Abu Pasang. His tall frame lowered itself out of habit through the kitchen door.

'Atung, check your phone, I recharged the internet pack an hour back. I called you several times!', he said without lifting his eyes off the phone. Atung Yeshi let out a soft joyful shriek. She explained how she was occupied with Anu from Delhi and had forgotten her phone in the bedroom. This excitement over the internet did not resonate with her husband, Aka Rinchin, who disliked her obsession with her phone and how it affected her sleeping pattern. 'This non-stop playing with phone is a new pandemic! She sleeps only after the rooster calls these days! Anyway, look how tall our Anu Norbu has grown!' Pasang looked away from his phone for the first time and his face brightened.

'Arre Anu! When did you come? So big you have gotten and beautiful also!'

Norbu blushed. Cousin or not, a good-looking young man's approval always triggered a mixture of embarrassment and triumph in her. Her community was not known for their political correctness and reticence especially with regard to aesthetics. There were people who were condemned to lifelong nicknames based on their physical appearance. An example was her cousin Nima Wangmu who was a slim, jovial woman in her late thirties. Norbu called her Anu. But she was known as Moti Anu by everyone despite her slim frame. She lost all the baby weight in high school but the name endured. To remark on someone's weight, complexion of skin, alignment of teeth was not considered out of line.

Pasang was leaving for Morshing, a village just a few miles away from Sethu. His sister had married a man from there three months ago. He had to collect the yak *chura* that she had bought from a Bhutanese chura trader two days ago. Norbu asked if he could drop her home on the way. She had had enough socializing for the day and needed to head home. She took her leave from her Aka and Atung but not before they thrust 1000 rupees in her hand and filled her little satchel with popcorn. She refused multiple times, following her mother's instructions, before accepting the material blessings graciously. To accept without resistance would betray a sign of greed or worse, impoverishment; to refuse would mean to challenge the elder's social rank.

Norbu had to stop at a shop on the highway to buy some milk powder for her father's morning tea. She never understood what the shiny, fat cows loitering in the village were for if not their milk. Beef was not as staple as fish and chicken and currently the village was under a curse according to the latest cosmological news mediated by the monks. 'Excessive bad karma,' they informed the villagers. 'We are Buddhist; we must stop killing,' they warned. A period of forced vegetarianism was imposed on the village, however those who really could not do without meat had to go to the nearby town which was at least two hours away by car to complete their daily victuals. Norbu saw no sin in milking the cows, perhaps the owners were not too keen on monetizing the dairy products of their livestock and kept the milk and cheese for themselves. After all there was so much one could do with milk. Norbu's thoughts on local commerce were as ephemeral as her cousin's cigarette smoke. Pasang had five minutes to finish his smoke before reaching his uncle's front gate. The wind also lent its hand to his clandestine habit.

'It would have been so much better if it were dark.'

Norbu couldn't hear Pasang; the motorcycle was slicing through the air making the wind whistle in her ears, but she felt his back vibrate.

'What?' (City voice).

'WHAT?' she repeated.

'I wish it was dark.'

'WHY?' Was there a fun event that happened at night that she didn't or wasn't supposed to know about? She was curious.

'Cause people would mistake my lit cigarette for a *zekmu*!' He roared with laughter, tickled by his witty humour.

'A WHAT?'

He lifted his veiny hand, where the cigarette was elegantly hanging between his surprisingly slim and delicate fingers and shook it lightly. 'A zekmu…ZEKMU oh!'

'Zekmuo?'

Pasang dropped an inquisitive Norbu to her father's gate and zoomed along the course of the road to Morshing. Norbu couldn't contain her fascination with the new knowledge; she ran to the kitchen to find her mother and Atung Pema sitting around the burning hearth, sipping black tea. Atung Pema had come to help around the house for their short stay in the village. Norbu's father had not bothered to include her husband's name in the tree of concerned members of the clan; she was merely told that her name is Atung Pema. Norbu started as soon as she entered, 'What is a zekmu, Atung?'

'Who told you about zekmus?' her mother inquired.

'Abu Pasang said zekmus are witches, *daayan*, *boksi* Ama!' She wished these synonyms would convince her mother to take her seriously. The Nepali equivalent was inserted intentionally to encourage her Nepali mother to conspire the contents of a supernatural legend through the solidarity of a shared vocabulary. She had seen her mother do it with other female relatives; their friendship always appeared to have grown deeper after some gossip.

'There are no such things as boksis. No.'

Norbu was about to protest when Atung Pema started talking in her soft voice. Her impassive tone belied the content of her speech.

'Zekmus are cursed women who sleepwalk. They leave a trail of blue flame as they fly across hills in the dead of the night, when everyone is asleep; even the crickets fall silent then.'

'Shut up, Anu!' Her mother hissed at Atung Pema. 'If you fill her mind with all this nonsense, she won't be able to sleep alone or even go to the toilet alone at night! Then I will have sleepless nights!' Her mother turned to Norbu and told her that zekmus and boksis were ancient stories told to entertain children or scare them, depending on the intellect of the child.

'Are you so simple as to think such things exist? Don't we send you to a good school? Didn't you learn anything from modern science?' Truth be told, ghosts and witches were never discussed in Norbu's school. There was a Holy Spirit though that appeared in the Headmaster's morning sermons. But this spirit seemed to be a good one, actually better than the village deity, more powerful than Guru Padmasabhava and even Buddha himself. This Holy Spirit could call their gods sinful and get away with it. So it would be safe to say that her school was equivocal in matters of the supernatural and the paranormal, but she kept this to herself. She was, after all, not that simple-minded. Her mother sent her to the bedroom to take a nap after lunch. Norbu decided to talk to her cousin about it later in the day, away from her mother's unyielding presence.

'They are kind of born with it…I don't think they are aware about their condition,' Tenzin, Norbu's first cousin thought out loud. She was three years older than Norbu. She lacked academic interest but was tremendously imaginative, adept at household chores and a state level volleyball player. She had lived in Sethu all her life and had had her first period that January, thus evidently becoming Norbu's confidant and mentor in matters of village life and questions of womanhood. The two girls were sitting on the porch of Tenzin's house which shared a wall with Norbu's. Her uncle, Aka Chandu had invited her family to dinner. Her father was excited to make his children taste his favourite dish from childhood, *pitto* but the children were actually looking forward to the juicy pork momos that their aunt, Tenzin's beautiful mother, made. She was Tibetan; her father had settled in a neighbouring village many decades back. The villagers characteristically gave her a literal name, Sundori, beautiful in Arunachali Hindi. Atung Sundori had an air of elegance around her; she had a slim long nose and high cheekbones, and despite her lack of formal education she seemed to be shrouded in worldly wisdom. Tenzin had taken after her father, with a round amicable face, dimples and an impelling need to talk. Her uninhibited chattiness often exposed her to ridicule. Many doubted the girl's intellectual capacity but if one observed her skilfully gut a fish or catch a volleyball right before it touched the ground as did Norbu, they wouldn't have judged her so harshly.

'Oh poor things! And they suffer all this stigma for no fault of their own!' Norbu exclaimed in a low voice.

'Of course not, I think they do know about their condition. They know who hurt them the previous night, so they go to that man the next morning. If the man who beat them the night before blows on their wounds, they are relieved of their pain immediately.' This confounding new information made

Norbu wonder what an awkward situation that would be for both the victim and the perpetrator. They heard Atung Sundori calling them for dinner.

Everyone sat around the burning hearth. The mothers seated themselves next to the hearth to keep the food from burning and seeing that everybody gets at least a second serving before their plates get empty. The fathers sat on the other side of the hearth, preparing pitto and sipping the whisky bought from the army shop in the neighbouring town. They pressed the buckwheat dough between their palms and then rolled it into pasta-like noodles. Later, the rolled noodles would be mixed with red chilli paste and fermented yak cheese and then dressed with a colourful salad made up of wild roots and herbs. They switched between Hindi and Sherdukpen as if to include their wives but, more importantly, to prevent the women from misunderstanding their conversation to be their disparagement. The three boys, Norbu's brother and Tenzin's twin brothers, reluctantly huddled together next to their fathers. Norbu's father had to stand at the door of the twins' bedroom to stop them from playing their playstation and come for dinner. They ate as quickly as possible to save time and optimally use the rest of it before another power cut. Norbu ate slowly as always; the pitto was underwhelming but in order to maintain the status of the favourite child she feigned delight in the dry dish. The momos obviously were magnificent. However, her mind mixed the flavoured oils of the fillings of the dumplings with her now prodigious curiosity about flying witches. As if she read her cousin's mind, Tenzin announced that Norbu had been asking her about zekmus and she knew nothing about them. She implored her parents to help her. The blissful cloud of minced meat and fantastical women vanished like smoke from Norbu's mind and she apologetically glanced at her mother, who met her with a stare which could only mean a predictably painful night for Norbu.

Her father's laughter interrupted her mother's glare. A reassuring roar that resounded in the warm kitchen. He went on to explain that such things didn't exist anymore but he remembered the time when he saw flying blue flames in the sky once when he was in school. Aka Chandu evidenced her father's claim with his own memory. 'I have seen a couple of them too. When we were in school, our toilets were outside, so midnight leaks also meant seeing these things.'

'Can you beat them up when you see them? They are not like spirits?' Norbu mustered some courage against her mother's tyrannical gaze. She wanted to make the most out of the situation before her inevitable punishment.

Her aunt, Atung Sundori, answered this time, 'I have heard that some of our older shamans did catch them loitering about at night and beat them with sticks and stones or whatever they could reach. In the morning the woman would be totally normal but completely bruised. She would go to the shaman's house and request him, "Oh grandfather, I won't make the same mistake; please blow on my wounds!"'

'Don't the rich ones fly on chests and the poor ones on brooms?'

'And the middle-class ones would fly on vacuum cleaners?' Norbu's mother retorted, interrupting the flow of an uncynical discussion.

This time it was Aka Chandu's turn to intervene, he always managed to relax Norbu's hard-nosed mother with his disarming charm, 'Arre Azu these are old stories but they were real in those days.' Turning to Norbu and Tenzin he continued, 'Zekmus fly on a box or broom depending on how rich or poor they are and congregate in a specific spot after midnight. They leave a pale blue trail in the sky. All the zekmus from across the land gather and they...'

'Gamble! They gamble their belongings, property and then eventually their husband's and children's lives. The ones riding on chests bring a lot of wealth to their family. But if they lose the gamble, it also means they might lose their children and husband. The stakes are high!' Norbu's father finished what Aka Chandu wanted to say, 'Yes, a lot of them end up alone; they do more harm to their own family than to others. Remember, that grandmother of ours, Abu? She looked very normal during the day but to think that she could venture out in the dead of night! And bet her husband's life; they were childless anyway. I wonder if her being a zekmu had anything to do with it...'

'Imagine having a zekmu for a wife or a mother? But then she was cursed to bet her family's wellbeing.' Atung Sundori mused sympathetically.

'Which grandmother?' asked Tenzin.

'Aah she is long dead now, doesn't matter.' Aka Chandu shrugged.

Norbu wondered if this tactile occult left any trace on its progeny. She thought to herself, was the zekmu's cursed addiction to gambling hereditary? She imagined a different kind of family tree now, one tied not to the male blood, surnames, land and rituals but one that swam through the blood of the zekmu. Would the zekmu's great granddaughter carry the same perverse line of magical powers that eventually consumed her and her family? It was clear to Norbu that a zekmu's biggest stake is the loss of a family and community. Can this loss invade the lives of her future generations? Her cousin, Kesang, interrupted her wild imagination with an intolerant rationality, 'You do know, it's methane right?' Everyone turned to the older twin who was on the edge of polite composure. He was tired of urban visitors including his city bred relatives who could only see the mystical in their culture without ever labouring the mundane everyday of this village. They always overlooked how modern and developed they had become and how much more was required. 'We used to collect livestock dung outside our homes then, for manure and fuel. The methane gas generated in those pits sometimes burst into blue flames! People didn't know any better those days!'

'So how did the flames reach the streets and the sky?' shot his mother.

'There are no zekmus anymore because there is light even at night now. Because of radio and TV and phone we don't sleep at night much, making it impossible for them to leave their homes, so now they are all gone.' Norbu's father concluded with finality. The night moved on to more prudent topics, about peach and kiwi farms and a prospective winery business. Whisky and rice beer were poured in abundance. Norbu eventually fell asleep with her head resting on her father's thigh and her younger brother Lakpa cried himself to sleep in his mother's lap after losing ten consecutive games to his older cousins. The zekmu had retreated into oblivion, at least for the night for everyone.

She fought herself awake from a strange dream. She was on the river bank; its wild water clamoured as if piercing through the land to divide it into two halves. She turned to find her family laughing under the thorny jabrang trees, cooking a meal on firewood across the river. Abu Pasang, her cousin with veiny forearms and delicate fingers, met her gaze and gestured to her to come to their side. She cupped both her hands around her mouth to amplify her city voice. They couldn't hear her. When she could finally have her mother's attention, her mother seemed to be mouthing something. The sound couldn't reach Norbu. They called her in desperation, her father, Tenzin, Aka Rinchin, Aka Chandu, but she could only see their mouths open and close frantically as if the river drowned their voices into its own cadence to an invisible ocean.

She broke herself out of the dream and opened her eyes to see nothing but darkness. She could hear her mother's rhythmic breathing. Norbu turned to her mother's side and placed her head under her armpit. Her warm body slowly diminished the afflictions of the nightmare. Norbu's ears pricked with attention to the sounds of the night. The stridulating crickets and other nocturnal beings were boldly claiming the night. And without any warning, the cricket suddenly stopped rubbing its wings and a blanket of silence fell around her. She tried to cover the silence with the sound of her own breath by breathing loudly and quickly and squeezed her eyes shut. Even the gentle glow of a firefly could have been fatal for Norbu's weak heart and the paranoia it revealed only in darkness. She couldn't remember when she fell asleep.

She woke up to the sound of matching footsteps. With light comes courage and rationality. It was the sound of shoes on gravel. The young cadets from the paramilitary force, which had stationed one of its battalions in the village a few years ago, were on their morning run. 'Even this leaves no time for the zekmu to fly freely on her brooms and her boxes,' she thought to herself. Maybe the zekmu was scared to be beaten by a battalion of soldiers trained in brutality. Perhaps, the zekmu too, like Atung Yeshi, had developed a new kind of insomnia. There was more than one reason for a zekmu to abandon her nocturnal tours. There was nothing to be afraid of now, thought Norbu. She decided to sleep better that night, and with that resolve she got out of the bed and went to the kitchen. Atung Pema was sweeping the cold ashes from the night before.

'The old ashes prevent the new fire from kindling, but we can use them to clean the brass utensils; they will shine like gold, you'll see! Fetch me some water in the kettle, Norbu.'

Pema adeptly lit the fire for the day and put the kettle of water on the bukhari. She then moved to the gas stove to prepare the morning tea.

The Room and I

REBOM BELO

Translated by
GEDAK ANGU

When eyes are awake
from break of dawn
I find myself in the room.
Hustle and bustle everywhere,
A reflection of my life
scattered and all shattered.

Promising myself every night
tomorrow I shall amend,
tidy up the mess,
but when my eyes open again,
things are in the same state –
The room and I.

The truth bites,
I turn off the light.
The darkness frightens me
I turn on the light.
This game of on-and-off continues.
The room and I.

We giggle when I am happy.
Drench the pillows when I am sad.
That thought, that secret
hidden from the world we share,
and debate through hours and hours.
The room and I.

Return wearied by work.
A friend awaits with wide open arms.
I embrace it then embark to heaven.
The room and I.

Indigenous Tribal Languages of North East India
Strategies for Revitalization

TOKO ANU

A language is more than a mere collection of words used for communication. It is a way of expressing our emotions, our understanding of reality, a way of socializing and bonding with others who share the same language as ours. However, language is also a medium to pass on information from one generation to the next, for it acts as a catalyst for the human race on its journey forward in history.

Of the estimated 6,000 languages spoken in the world, the United Nations Educational, Scientific and Cultural Organisation (UNESCO) has identified around 43 per cent as 'endangered' or 'vulnerable'. It wouldn't be an overstatement to argue that a considerable number of languages from India's North East are gradually dying due to a number of factors. In fact, in Arunachal Pradesh, the Bugun and Sherdukpen languages have roughly 3,000 speakers and they are very likely the last generation of such speakers.

This was the significance of the 7th edition of the annual North East Festival held in New Delhi under the aegis of the Indira Gandhi National Centre for the Arts (IGNCA). The festival's theme was oral narratives and linguistic diversity in India. It is important to note that this took place at a time when the country and its multiple different languages are currently facing a risk of homogenization and consequent death at the hands of the ruling dispensation, and its efforts to establish a single language for the entire nation and its people. The festival organized panel discussions and symposiums on the loss of languages and the many possible strategies for their revitalization.

As an editor at the Indian Cultural Forum in New Delhi, I attended these sessions and interacted with several wonderful artists and writers from the North East, which gave me insights into their varied efforts in preserving the region's 'indigenous' cultures and languages. Here, I compile the insights I gained from various speakers on the important subject of the revitalization of indigenous tribal languages in the North East of India.

Building theories based on native parameters

At a symposium in Delhi titled 'Language Loss and Revitalization Strategies: Challenges for Indigenous people of North East India', Dr Hesheto Y. Chishi, Director of the Indigenous Cultural Society of Nagaland, recalled an incident where he was asked to write on the jewellery of the Naga tribe. After Dr Chishi handed in his essay, the scholar who had asked him to write said that the piece did not carry enough 'substance' because Chishi had not used references. Dr Chishi clarified that the work was based on primary data but the scholar was not convinced; the article then had to be archived and it was later published in the March 2019 edition of *Northeast Window*.

Dr Chishi's point was that mainstream academia in the country had not yet recognized the value of primary research. Instead, undue importance was given to theories based on generic research that have ended up 'theorizing' or stereotyping the North Easterners. It is high time the scholars of the region moved away from theories about us constructed by outsiders and built theories based on our own understanding of what is around us, that is, cultural narratives by the people of the region and not based on already existing academic research or theories alone. 'Culture' means 'to cultivate'. When we cultivate we begin by carefully preparing the earth for crops in order to promote growth. Thus, let us use native parametres to define our own culture.

The North East through 'orature'

Speaking on the extinction of indigenous languages and cultural change Dr Usham Rojio, academic councillor at IGNOU refuted the popular statement, 'when a language dies, a culture dies'. He argued that it is the death of a way of life that first leads to the disappearance of a certain knowledge system and along with that dies a language. The cultural hegemony of 'dominant' groups has created a binary opposition between the North East's tribal groups and mainstream society. The distinction between folk and classic, where folk is looked down upon while the 'classical' is revered, is an example of this. In Rojio's view, people in the North East are engaged in a process of emulation of the West or 'Westernization' and 'Brahmanization' (processes similar to the phenomenon of 'Sanskritization') to seek upward mobility in society, and this has led to the gradual extinction of their own tribal languages.

Borrowing from Kenyan writer and academic Ngũgĩ wa Thiong'o, Dr Rojio also said that the cultural practices of the North East are to be viewed as 'orature'. Defined as 'the oral equivalent of literature', orature is a knowledge system that is sufficient for a society to exist and function. Besides 'external manifestations' like performing arts, it also encompasses 'interior elements' of the culture, reflected in its core values. Dr Rojio is of the view that in the North East, each orature originated and developed within the context of the region's unique landscape. However, urbanization and modernization have not only altered this landscape, but have also depleted orature, causing a loss in the meanings specifically associated with it.

Referring to the Garo film, *My name is Eeooow*, which tells the story of a mother and her three sons who have the same name, each distinguished according to three different tonal vibrations of sound, he raised doubts about being able to accommodate such intricacies of orature in the present system. 'In order to exhibit the true meaning of orature,' Dr Rojio said, 'we need to look beyond folk performances in the metropolitan cities which can be counterproductive for they often end up exoticizing the culture of the North East.'

Beyond the Roman script

Dr Walinur Ao, an Associate Professor at Amity University, spoke at length about the damage the Roman script has done to the cultural expression of tribes in the North East. It is well known that many tribes in the region who do not have a script of their own extensively use the Roman script. 'Although unintended,' Dr Ao said, 'translation causes the loss of authentic, symbolic meaning of the language and culture.' Citing his research on Nagaland's Ao tribe, Dr Ao said, 'Translation is re-representation and not an actual presentation. It compromises on the meaning of words.' To illustrate this, he said that the single word 'wash' in Ao has several variations, according to the different contexts and tones in which the word was pronounced. For example, 'shitok' refers to washing clothes, 'meit' to washing feet, 'metsuk' to washing hands, 'alok' to washing hair, 'meiyi' means to wash the face.

In fact, not having a script did not deter Banwang Losu, a researcher in Linguistics at Pune's Deccan College (Post Graduate and Research Institute) in his efforts to save Wancho, a language on the verge of extinction in Arunachal Pradesh. Through painstaking research over twelve years, Losu developed a new Wancho script using the International Phonetic Alphabet (IPA), an alphabetic system of phonetic notation based primarily on the Latin alphabet. In an interview with the Indian Cultural Forum[1] Losu said that as a language enthusiast, he realized that the Roman script was not a suitable alternative for the tribal languages of the

[1] https://indianculturalforum.in/2019/10/21/birth-of-the-wangcho-script-an-effort-to-preserve-arunachal-pradeshs-wangcho-culture/

North East. He felt it overlooked the many tones, words and phrases of the region's languages. The meanings of words were derived not simply from words alone but also from the particular tone and pitch used while pronouncing them. Losu added that other tribes of the region should also develop their own scripts and thereby give up the use of the Roman script, which was not capable of capturing the many nuances of the region's languages. The new Wancho script is now being implemented in the curricula of around thirty schools in Arunachal Pradesh's Longding district.

Redesigning school curricula

In its June 2019 report, *Mother Tongue Matters: Local Language as a Key to Effective Learning*, UNESCO establishes that a child's first language is the most effective medium of learning throughout his/her primary education. In spite of this, many parents in the North East insist that their children learn English or languages considered 'regionally privileged'.

Citing her research, 'Language Loss, Strategies and Revitalization: A Karbi Perspective' at the symposium, academic Dr Maggie Katharpi identified the non-inclusion of local tribal languages in the school curricula as one of the primary factors for the near-death state of indigenous languages in the region. Substantiating her argument, she said that she was appalled to know that the Karbi language was not recognized as a 'standard language' by the state board or the National Council of Educational Research and Training (NCERT) in the schools of the Karbi-Anglong district of Assam, mostly inhabited by the Karbi-speaking Karbi tribe.

Dr Prachee Dewri spoke of the need to redesign the curricula of schools in the North East and on the 'cognitive dissonance' experienced by Deori children. 'The Anglicized representations of families in textbooks make it difficult for the children to relate to their own family,' said Dewri. Sounding a warning about the ill effects of forced language transition in schools, Dr Dewri and Dr Katharpi said this signalled the risk of children losing the ability to connect with their cultural heritage and becoming linguistically incompetent in the future. This would, in their opinion, lead to a gradual depletion of the indigenous repository of languages, dialects and knowledge systems carried through them.

The solution should come from within communities, in order to prevent further damage. 'Instructions from above' on cultural preservation have not been very helpful, according to the academics. 'Real efforts' include measures such as redesigning school curricula based on realistic representations of the societies the children belong to and the use of the mother tongue as the medium of instruction in schools.

Dr Chishi and Dr Aò were also of the view that the government had to promote the policy of 'parents as first teachers', for children look up to their parents and use their actions to make sense of the world around them. They added that no amount of formal education on culture could compare with the influence parents had on their children, especially in the early stages of their growth.

Reassessing school uniforms

The symposium also discussed the importance of local attire as expressions of a community's identity. Dr Ao emphasized the importance of using traditional attire as school uniforms in the North East. He said that these were external manifestations of people's social identities, origins and allegiances. Attire had an important symbolic role in the preservation of cultural heritage and distinctiveness. 'Introducing the practice of wearing traditional dress as uniform at least a few days a week in schools will create a sense of belonging among the students,' said Ao. 'In a way, it is a confidence building measure among students who have associated schools with western learning while discounting their own indigenous heritage.' Dr Chishi added to this by arguing that wearing traditional dresses as school uniforms was important in order to create a positive environment in schools, for such practices created a link between the complex dichotomies of modernity versus tradition.

Cultural diplomacy

Since their debut in 2013, the South Korean pop music group BTS, or the Bangtan Boys, has not only become an international sensation but has also been active in spreading contemporary Korean culture across the globe. BTS has become a driving force of 'people-to-people' diplomacy in spreading soft power and changing the perception of what it is to be 'Korean' across the world. At the festival, Dr Chishi stressed the importance of cultural diplomacy and spoke on how one could learn from South Korea's use of soft power.

As an editor at the Indian Cultural Forum, I have come across and interacted with artists from the North East who deserve praise for similar efforts. The 25-member Shillong Chamber Choir performed parts of 'Sohlyngngem', an opera in Khasi, at the popular *MTV* India Music Summit held in Jaipur as a tribute to the language. In my interview with their lead vocalist, William Richmond Basaiawmoit, he said that the group had been performing operas in Italian, French and many other Western languages, and when the thought of performing a Khasi opera struck, they simply decided to make it happen. Basaiawmoit said that this was because Khasi as a language is not only rich in folklore but has gentle, soft vowels and consonants that work perfectly for operas. The opera received an amazing response at the summit. According to him, an artist at the summit even volunteered to learn Khasi and perform in the language to inspire others to work towards the preservation of this vulnerable tribal language. 'Opera is more in-depth and provides an aesthetic, emotional experience unlike any other. When people hear that an opera will be performed in Khasi, it will certainly stir an interest about the language itself among its listeners,' said the singer.

In his efforts to blend contemporary music with traditional folklore, David Angu, the lead vocalist of the rock band Soul of Phoenix, started the project 'David Angu & the Tribe'. 'Ho Delo', the project's debut production was released on YouTube in October 2019 and it received more than 500 views on the first day. In an interview with me David said,

> Folktales are a rich database of traditional wisdom on life that our ancestors left for us. The older generation in my native village, Angu (West Siang district), sing Galo folktales to teach children. It is the melody that makes children take an interest in this traditional knowledge. So, after playing classic rock and glam rock for a few years, I decided to blend modern rock with traditional tribal folklore. That is when I

started David Angu & the Tribe. The project is dedicated to exploring tribal folk melodies of Arunachal Pradesh's tribes and playing them in a modern musical style the younger generation prefers.

As the foundation of cultural diplomacy, the use of soft power to promote the 'indigenous' on the international stages is an excellent strategy to mobilize cultural resources and build opinions and associations based on the region's culture and values.

The current language policy

Governments in the North East have a considerable influence on the daily lives of people in the region. Much of the administrative work of the government is carried out in what are known as the 'official' languages. At the conference Dr Chishi suggested that it was important to reconsider these 'official' languages. According to him, the existing language policy hindered the development of local languages. Instead, each state needed to have two different types of official languages – those that were general and then those what were district-specific. Since every state in the region has multiple tribes and each tribe has a unique language, the tribal language of a particular district should be declared its official language, along with English. This led to a discussion on the dangers of the 'One Nation, One Language' policy. Dr Rojio added here that it was important that India's diversity be respected and preserved, else the policies and attitudes of the current government would lead to the slow death of the country's myriad languages. Dr Lianboi Vaiphei, who teaches at Indraprastha College in Delhi, spoke of the threat the extensive use of English posed to North East India's tribal languages and added that the use of the dialects of a specific area/village's dominant class can also discreetly kill the smaller tribal dialects of the area. An example was the use of Meiteilon by the tribals of Manipur.

Documentation and timely revision

The need to document folk cultures and traditional knowledge systems also came in for discussion. Dr Ao addressed the use of audio-visual digitization to preserve and disseminate. The idea behind setting up a digital archive of the North East was that it would also be possible for the rest of the world to access this knowledge, thus Dr Ao advocated both documentation and research, and emphasized that they should be facilitated and promoted.

Culture and language are not static but fluid and complex, thus it is important, as emphasized by Dr Chishi, to look at the dynamics of language. The ways in which human beings communicate change over time and languages are continually renewed and reshaped as they come in contact with other languages and cultures. The Oxford English Dictionary, for example, updates its content on a quarterly basis. Chishi suggested that similar practices of updating and review should be followed while documenting and standardizing indigenous cultural practices.

In conclusion, I suggest that language is not only a means of communication, but also a vehicle to pass down a community's heritage to its future generations, and indeed a way for communities to claim their identity. Versatile as they are, languages are bound to change, adapt and evolve over time. My intention in presenting the discussions above goes beyond the simple promotion of tribal languages in the North East, rather, I am interested in finding ways to build confidence among the people of the region to be able to undo the damage of cultural hegemony we have suffered at the hands of dominant groups. It is important that we change the perception of the 'indigenous', which is often viewed as part of a 'little tradition', and look at such attempts to preserve indigenous traditions as movements to assert the right to be who we are and fight to 'dis-label' the indigenous as 'raw', 'crude' and 'unrefined'. Our attempts should be to re-evaluate the orature of the North East and explore the treasure of knowledge it has to offer.

Some may argue that going back to the past is not a viable solution. While that is largely true, it should not be misunderstood as suggesting that we discard modernization and return to some state of being 'primitive'. The idea is to bring back and retain the region's distinct identities in a rapidly globalizing world. The attempt is to create a sense of belonging to one's indigenous identity without compromising the values of modernity.

Those Idle Days

JAMUNA BINI

Translated from Hindi by
YATER NYOKIR

I remember
to this day
those idle days
of my early years.

Swinging my tiny feet
over the Jhumkheti Phurup
and eating cucumber

Far down Appa chasing goats in the playing field
defending maize, paddy and millet.

The dancing beat of my will,
sometimes dragging me to play a part in their daily
    grind,
sometimes dragging me to sleep all day long.

My indolence irked Appa
but wayward me
lost in a world of my own,
weaving cheerful dreams,
admiring the lively gaze of colourful butterflies
playing hide and seek in the emerald meadows of
    paddy.

While Appa
tangled with rowdy beasts in her acre,
bereft of this joyous sight of
the flickering play of butterflies.

In the distant inky grey,
when the sun folds its golden rays
my tender fingers holding Appa's soil-stained hands
matching her practiced limbs
descending towards home
down the slippery slope.

Fumes of granny's tobacco
in the air of the courtyard,
Inside, a roaring fire dancing in the hearth.
This is my Namda,
the biggest house of the village.

In this bamboo house
when the fourteen hearths
blaze in tune
the floating flames swim through the bamboo cracks
and brighten up the world outside.

Around these hearths folks circle the fireplace,
feast and recount anecdotes,
soon to fall asleep
for tomorrow at crack of dawn
they will rouse themselves again
to journey to their distant fields.

Today
these hearths are broken.
Folks no more live together.
Seeking opportunities and knowledge
they depart towards the cities
deserting the smiling village.

Now
We don't live in bamboo houses anymore,
no more do fires glow through the cracks of those
    bamboo houses.
Our houses are made of concrete now.
Our nights are stretched
sunk in our laptops, mobiles and TV,
SMS, Facebook and WhatsApp have
became the medium of our bonds.

The Darkest 5 Days

TOLUM CHUMCHUM

There you show up again redhead, huh?
Blossoming on my sheets
Like a barrel of red wine
Between my legs
I must wake before the sun for the rosy laundry
'For woman you have become' said my mother
My stomach bloats
My head throbs
My limbs ache
The cry of my body
Like a cooking show going, on my belly;
Burn, chop, blend, swinging my bloody mood
My abdomen seems like a piece of dough
Punch, twist, turns and cramps
When you travel down my fallopian
Please! Mercy on my uterus,
Discomfort in groups
Distraction in class

Which birth vengeance is this pain for?
How long must I endure
Answer me, dear darkest 5 days of the month

Evocation

CHASOOM BOSAI

I have a beautiful memory
Of a place, of an echo
The sublime world, the enchanted valley!
Of the voice that still whispers like it used to.
Of memories that have a home
Built in dreams. Built with love
Of the days when it didn't matter
how scorching the sun was.
Or how heavy the rain used to be
And how late nights would be.

Thousand days apart, the rose still blooms
Miles apart, the sun still sets
Million dreams dreamed, the moon still shines bright.
The words swallowed but I still write
I write not to you, I write to nobody
I write for the memories lived
I write for the uproar

Deep in my heart, within me
But yes I have a memory, a beautiful one
Of a place, of an echo
And that – I will adore
this beautiful evocation.

The Spirit of the Forest

SUBI TABA

On the outskirts of the hilly foothills of the eastern Himalayas, in an isolated town named Seijosa, a newly-appointed Range Forest Officer drove his jeep into the untouched dense native ecosystem of the Pakke Tiger Reserve, an area that stretched across eight hundred kilometers of Pakke Kessang district of western Arunachal. The jeep grumbled over the stony road, scaring some little ringed plovers that scattered away in swift flights towards the riverside. The quiet old town existed near the buffer zone of the tiger reserve with a few linear village settlements near the roadside, enveloped by the arms of the dense semi-evergreen forests. The new officer settled into his office-cum-home in the middle of the forest, accompanied by a colony of forest guard barracks and a lone standing tourist lodge which remained unoccupied most of the seasons, except for the caretaker and the cook, who remained drunk most nights. The Pakke river flowed in a murmuring permanence at some distance, bordering the village and the tiger reserve.

In the forest, the last crowing of the jungle fowls indicated that it was time for sundown vigilance by the forest guards. As the sun disappeared behind the giant tall trees, the forest grew animated. Each sound magnified as the night deepened. The whispers of the wind could incite any weak mind into fearful hallucinations. The singing cicadas made the forest sound like it was in a rhythmic dance, wearing anklet bells. The slow hooting of the owls sounded like a spirit lurking behind the tall tree, waiting to play hide and seek. The buzzing of mosquitoes, seemingly denouncing the world, could turn any living thing into a malarial madness.

One moonlit night, deep in the forests, the rustling of the leaves grew louder, and was followed by hurried footsteps. A wild boar was running frantically for his life. Three men, each armed with a dagger, a spear and a gun were chasing the boar in the jungle, pushing aside the hanging trees and bushes. The first gunshot hit the boar in the back, rupturing its skeletal system. The boar fell abruptly, unable to run. The forest grew silent. *It was a defeat.* The barking deer ran and hid in the bushes; a gaur woke up from his sleep at the sound of the gunshot; the pied wart frog momentarily stopped croaking his monotonous mating call; a solitary clouded leopard climbed up a tall Tetrameles tree to spy on the nocturnal sentience of the forest. The officer and the guards heard the sound of the gunshot. They jumped into the jeep and headed towards the source of the sound.

The three armed men gingerly stepped towards the motionless boar, which was bleeding from the back.

'It's dead!' The man with the gun whispered as he slowly lowered himself next to the animal, closely pointing the gun at it and lightly prodding the motionless body with the muzzle. The other two men stood warily in their hunting stances, shining their torches on the frozen boar. As the first man leaned down to grab the body, the wild boar jumped up suddenly and ploughed his head into the man's chest, attacking with all the strength left in its neck muscles, pinning the man down on the ground.

'It's alive!' The man with the dagger cried in panic and jumped up onto a small tree, fearing for his life. He hung on to its feeble branches.

The attacked man wrestled with the boar, his eyes meeting the animal's small, deep-set eyes, which stared right at him with vengeance. The man tried with all his might to push away the boar with his hand and at that very moment realized that a wild boar, though small in size, had the strength to disfigure a human body. The boar caught hold of the man's hand in his mouth and with its well developed canine teeth, crunched into the flesh and bones of the man. A loud painful cry escaped the man's throat. He cried for help as he tried to kick the boar away but was unable to rescue his hand. The other man jabbed his spear into the boar, puncturing its neck and managed to shove it aside. The boar collapsed and died, the man's hand intact inside his mouth.

The forest mourned the death of the wild boar and came alive with a cacophony of shrieking animals and birds. The arrival of the officer's jeep threw light on the man, who was lying bloodied with broken ribs and a missing hand. The other poachers were arrested while the injured man was taken to the hospital where he lay in a coma for many months, only seeing the dreadful faces of animal spirits.

On a sunny day, in the northern side of the protected forest, the oldest and mightiest trees fell down in creaking anguish as labourers seared the trunks with sharp blades. They had been hired by a man who had fraudulently encroached on the protected land. The man was a rich ex-minister who made tall promises to the village dwellers during the elections only to drain all their money into his account. For the village, the promised developments never arrived; the roads were never built, the offices never renovated, the connectivity never started, the electricity never connected and the schemes never implemented. The only development that happened was an exponential increase in his personal wealth – thousands of hectares of illegal land acquisition, crores of business investments in the cities, a king-sized villa with a swimming pool and all kinds of luxuries. Meanwhile, the village remained poor and its inhabitants led a quiet miserable life.

Mr Fraudulent sat on a folding chair, a drink in his hand, with a big sun hat and dark sunglasses, ordering the labourers to clear the forest. He lived a life of luxury while the labourers worked all day and lived in shabby barracks barely held together with sodden planks of wood. He was the only rich man in the village and his villa was the touristy talk among the villagers, for only a few privileged ones had ever been inside.

The mighty old trees, which were natural homes for the forest birds and animals, were destroyed and laid down as logs, conveyed to a saw mill and neatly cut into rectangular pieces, which were placed on transport trucks for a business detour to the markets of Assam. The truck consignments were sent stealthily at night when the forest check gate guards were asleep on duty or open to communication with money. In the village, the most congenial wordless communication

Mr Fraudulent had mastered was through money. The villagers and some crooked officials proudly took the money as they did not have other resources to live an entertaining life in the wild.

When he heard the news about the illegal tree felling, the RFO decided to pay a visit to Mr Fraudulent. The officer was astonished to see a magnificent villa standing in the village. It seemed almost unreal to see something like that standing in the middle of such a modest village.

'So, you are the new Ranger who has not become acquainted with me yet?' Mr Fraudulent asked in a loud voice as he studied the officer with his shrewd eyes. The officer observed the massive chandelier hanging over the hall, the glossy marble floor with intricate designs and the aristocratic indoor furnishings. Mr Fraudulent's eyes followed the officer's gaze and mentioned, 'It's all imported from Dubai, you see.' He called for his new wife to greet the officer. The new, young wife served tea and biscuits.

'Sir, I came to give you an order to stop felling trees in the protected wildlife area,' the officer solemnly said, avoiding mundane talks as he handed over the order.

Mr Fraudulent's face turned pink as he read the official order letter with bloodshot eyes.

'You don't know me yet!' Mr Fraudulent gritted his teeth. 'I am the boss of this land, the river, the sky and the forest! I can do anything I like with it! Who are you to issue me an order letter for illegal forest felling, huh? I can get you transferred or suspended in the snap of a finger with my higher authority link ups!' He threw the order paper up in the air.

'Sir, I am just doing my duty,' the officer answered calmly.

'Why, haven't you tasted the sweetness of money like the other rangers yet?' Mr Fraudulent hissed, producing a bubble of spit in between his lips.

The officer chuckled at Mr Fraudulent's proposition of bribery. He stood up, the tea untouched, and he wandered around looking at the furnishings of the villa and then offered, in friendly ridicule, 'It looks like you have sucked all the public money for the development of the village into this soulless villa of yours!'

'How dare you? You small grade officer!' Mr Fraudulent's temper raged and he paced up and down, then he rushed and grabbed a gun hanging on the wall. The new wife cried out and stopped him.

The officer stood motionless, startled by the wild animosity of the man, and he wondered whether the man wanted to scare him or shoot him with the gun. He adjusted his uniform cap and walked out of the villa with great disquiet in his mind but pretended to be unaffected.

'If you and your forest department try to stop me, I am going to burn down your whole forest and its useless animals!' Mr Fraudulent yelled from the doorway.

The officer got into his jeep and rode away, pondering how to handle the situation and deal with the greedy man. He ordered the forest guards to stay alert in their respective camps and also wrote a few applications to the higher officials, which fell on deaf ears and lay static under layers of pending government office files.

The tree felling continued for months, terrorizing the forest people and animals. The family of Rhesus monkeys, capped langurs, weasles, the mongoose, squirrels and porcupines migrated to the central part of the forest. A wreathed hornbill father, who had set out to forage food for his female and chick sealed inside a tree trunk, could not locate the tree anymore. Wild boars foraging for wild roots dispersed into the deforested vicinity and were mercilessly chased by the labourers. The natural harmony of the forest was disturbed.

Once the tree felling in the northern side was accomplished, the sinister mind of Mr Fraudulent didn't stop. His ego craved for more destruction. He called one of his labourers and communicated to him in cash, pointing his fingers towards the forest. That night, the deforested area caught fire. Dried leaves and stems caught fire, cracking into fierce flames and lighting up the forest. Mr Fraudulent looked at the tongues of flame in the distance from his villa terrace and sneered in his black heart.

The officer and the guards were in the anti-poaching camp inside the forest, when they heard the muffled outcry of birds and animals. The night owls hooted hysterically. They stood up from their tea breaks and looked into the horizon of the night sky. They saw the blazing fire light up the sky, and called out an alarmed warning call, 'Wildfire! Wildfire!' They quickly climbed down the jungle tree house, which was built at a height of six metres to avoid confrontation with elephants and other wild animals. They armed themselves with guns and ran through the forest in the small foot trails. There was a hullabaloo in the forest. Only when they were deep in the forest did they realize that human survival skills narrowed down to zero in the presence of the mighty darkness of the wild. They had hair raising experiences as they watched the animals in motion and stood still, huddled next to the trunk of a mighty Banyan tree as the animals and birds they had never seen together at the same time all stormed past them.

The elephants ran in herds in chaotic trumpeting, clouded leopards leaped furiously, capped langurs frantically swung forward grasping the branches of trees, Himalayan palm civets rushed, jackals howled, the Himalayan black bear growled, as they all ran away from the forest fire.

The officer fell down on his knees, heartbroken to see the fire ravaging the forest and spreading towards them. They were in the deep forest without phone signals and did not know how to ask for help. He remembered Mr Fraudulent's words and felt defeated that he couldn't do anything to protect the forest. That night he heard a searing angry female scream that rose with the forest flames up into the skies. And like a true miracle, there was loud angry thunder and a heavy streak of lightning that split up the sky. To his utter surprise, the clouds began to pour. He just sat open mouthed, watching water defeat fire. His eyes welled up applauding the marvellous works of nature. Some small animals and insects got burnt in the fire but most survived including bigger mammals and birds; some amphibians survived hiding in burrowed holes and sheltered rocks.

Once the fire died down, among the burnt ashes, a charred body of a man holding a petrol container was discovered by one of the guards who remarked, 'He went out to burn down the forest, but the forest burnt him down!' The body was identified as that of the labourer who worked for Mr Fraudulent.

Back in the village, there was a big fuss about the fire. The officer drove his jeep to the villa. A small gathering collected outside the villa with men and women with despairing faces and heads hung low. The officer walked in furiously, very aware that Mr Fraudulent had something to do with the fire.

Inside the villa, there was a funeral going on. The officer's anger mellowed when he saw a swarm of people saying their last goodbyes to a body wrapped in a white local shawl, covered with flowers and incense sticks. The officer took off his cap and walked towards the body. As he walked over and saw the face, his stomach turned. He was so shocked that he stumbled slightly. The face and body were coal black, charred to death. Even in the blackness, the officer could identify the face.

'How did he die?' One of the mourners asked the servant.

'He got struck by lightning while he was on the terrace last night.'

The new widow, eyes drenched with tears stood near the hall, thanking whoever had come. She saw the officer and thanked him for coming even though her husband hadn't been nice to him. The officer thought of saying something but decided to keep his words to himself and walked out of the villa after offering his condolences to the widow.

The village started to whisper about the cause of death of Mr Fraudulent. In the coming years this story would become an urban legend with each one at the mercy of their own conclusions. Some reasoned that he had died of the lightning shock. Others claimed that a female spirit living in the forest got enraged and burnt him down for destroying the forest. While some hypothesized that all the dead spirits of the forest animals and birds raced towards him to avenge their death and charred him to death along with them. Meanwhile, the officer drove back to his forest quarters believing that *love begets love, so does destruction beget destruction.*

The next morning the forest looked radiant and rejuvenated after the rain. The officer breathed in the fresh air and walked into the pathway trailing into the vast tranquility of the forest. There were reports to be written about the latest incident and duties to be assigned to the guards but he stood in the forest, his eyes resting on the web of mighty branches cradling the blue skies. In the distance he observed the pugmarks of a big cat on the wet soil and a short way away, like royalty, there stood a Bengal Tiger. The officer's breath stilled. No one had seen a tiger for a long time in the forest. The tiger looked at the officer silently, roared victoriously and slowly disappeared into the dense grove of the forest. A mighty flock of oriental pied hornbills rose over the dense canopy of the forest, a blue throated barbet flapped its wings and sang, perched on the tall tree, rousing and glorifying the spirit of the forest again.

Feels Like Something is Lacking

NOMI MAGA GUMRO

Translated by
TAGE MONI

Every time feels like something is lacking.
Every time feels like something is extinguished.
This poem of mine may not remain incomplete
That resides in the shelter of my heart.

Maybe those eyes were indicating something.
Maybe those sealed lips were saying something.
See the display of time
Conveying many things.

From the tip of a nib
Whatever could be penned today
Those words, those lines
Why are they silent today?

Maybe something is there?
which seems embedded in my heart.

This moment, this night
May be supporting me
to complete my lines.
Why then,
That satisfaction has not been achieved
That seems to be the obsession of this heart.

Every time feels like something is lacking.
Every time feels like something is extinguished.
This poem of mine may not remain incomplete
That resides in the shelter of my heart.

Tried being careless,
Tried being careful too.
My breath stops at that.
My way wanders, somewhere there.
Every time feels like something is lacking,
Every time these eyes seem to be moistened.

Lullaby

MISHIMBU MIRI

The Kera-aa Idu community believe in the concept and effect of the evil eye. The evil eye is said to be a curse cast by a malevolent glare falling upon a person – adult or child – when they are unaware of it. The lullaby is a protective measure against the evil eye, and is sung to children to protect them from being touched by it. It is also sung when a child falls sick. The lullaby is not sung by everyone in society, rather it is sung by both men and women who have knowledge of the language in which hymns and prayers are chanted. When the singer sings they give words spontaneously to thoughts that spring to the mind as they try to drive away the evil eye or to protect the child from the evil glare of the unknown.

Aa-aa tse, anjamina tse
Aade yemi miwu yaponjo-o ijumichi tse
Aa-aa-aahi yombrowu athutoo iwe aponjo injumichi tse
Aaa yomota shelo zinu meh tse,
Yomota mide layame ummm

Abü lano shelopru gawodoma iwu yaponji iju kena
Ummm....

This particular lullaby was sung by a priest, Srimati Dishi Rondo. It has more verses; their translation is as follows:

O! Little baby don't cry when the sun is setting.

Let your voice not be heard by the evils that are nearby during sunset.

If you are crying let it be a prayer for Eni Mashelo Zinu.

Let your voice be heard by the good spirits to carry it to the Almighty.

O! Sweet baby, don't cry. Let my lullaby sung for you be heard by the benevolent spirits of the house to protect you from evil. Let them shield you from bad omens and the evil glare.

O! Baby, let your voice plead with the benevolent spirits present in every nook and corner of the house to keep you safe. Let me sing you the blessing of the Almighty bestowed on you at birth.

Oh Lord! Let the cry of the baby be for a good cause and the baby's wellbeing. Let his voice not reach the ears of the evil spirits. Take him to your bosom; the soul of the baby must have been scared away by evil spirits. Oh! Lord, protect his soul and guide it back to his body.

Oh! The Almighty above, with your blessings let my words heal him. Bestow on me the powers to drive away the curse of the evil eye and to heal the baby. Let me sing to him of your glory. Lord, take him to your bosom and protect him from the evil spirits.

The lullabies sung in the Idu community do not have similar patterns or words. They can vary from person to person according to their understanding of the priestly language, and their content depends on who is singing. The lullaby can be sung by both priests and non-priests in the community. They can choose to offer prayers and seek blessings, or sing the glories of the ancestors of the baby and moral thoughts of the elders alongside offering prayers.

From: The *Reh Souvenir,* 2019

I Am Property
A Photo Essay

KARRY PADU

This photo essay bases itself on screen grabs of the Film 'I Am Property' made as part of the Zubaan-Sasakawa research grant (2019). When I first wrote the script sitting in my parents' house in Aalo town in West Siang district of Arunachal Pradesh, I watched myself looking over our quaint town and the growing signs of 'civilization' in it.

The traditional ornaments women wore, which came with age-old norms that dictated how women should behave, felt like such a heavy burden to be carried. They spoke only about the need for protection, or 'rights' under the guidance of a man.

I realized that as we grow up, we begin to understand the world around us. Our education and our exposure to the world start shaping our outlook on it. Perhaps this is what pushes us also to question the age-old norms which our tribal ancestors laid down for us. It is time we did so with strength in our questioning and our voices, for if we are hesitant, our voices will not be heard; they will be ignored.

1. *Threads of tradition*

When I was young, I had no idea how important it
  was to be a tribal woman,
How, so many threads of tradition bind you to
  customs and the tales of the ancestors.
I followed them for my ancestors – those learned men
  who laid them down!
I was born here in this land, I belong to this lands and
  its traditions.
I am its daughter, this land owns me.
I am its property!

2. No Questions, No Comparison

I never questioned anything before because it was normal, I never asked why things cannot change because how could I? How can I compare myself with the women who have fought for equal rights and for equal wages around the world?

How can I compare myself to women who are allowed to speak their minds?

My traditions are different, my customs are different.

3. My Value

I am weighted in numbers of cattle rather than gold.
I am a proud tribal woman, I respect my traditions.
I respect them for they make my tribe unique
I respect them because they make me who I am.

4. *Fear of questioning*

I fear them because the forces are stronger than me.
I fear a tribe who will be angry with me if I defy them.
I fear alienation,
I fear being an outcast,
I fear losing my faith if I dare question.
Moreover, even if I question,
Who will answer?

Little Life

DOIRANGSI KRI

Great is the joy and glee
Amazing is the grace of divine thee
Unique is the struggle and pain
Wonderful the ultimate gain

Three quarters of a year, you in me
Fed, kicked and frolicked in the space so free
You grew within, said they baby on board
The yoke of you and me through a navel cord

You stepped into the world with a cry
I turned towards you with a passionate sigh
All the cramps and gripe I bury
Your arrival bears off every worry

Your babbles, grunts, hiccups and chuckle
Your cry and laughter all are just a miracle
Neh, eh, heh and owh I hear
Sounds I love afar and near.

Pseudo Life

DOIRANGSI KRI

We live in a world, world just born
Discrete and novel from the one bygone
From hoary strife to the time of ease
Values and morals all seem to cease
Wonders of science and inventions at hand
Baffled is the world at the plethora of brands
Comfort, luxury and opulence each proclaim
All in an array of gaining name and fame
Transgressed are the ideals of simple living, high
    thinking
Gandhian ideals of equality and tolerance are
    shrinking
Holy Communion heading into mere wrangles
Trailing behind is camaraderie, states are lost in
    tangles
Beauty and power of learning is lost
All is gained online from internet's cost
Epics, legends and myths are no more pursued

On Facebook, WhatsApp and Insta all are glued
We talk of searing issues like climate change
We owe a future world, which will be strange
Heat is on the rise and our sphere so tainted
Will be tough for our earth to be repainted.

Linguistic Transitions

YANIAM CHUKHU

I remember speaking fluently in my mother tongue, Nyishi, during my childhood. This was before I was sufficiently exposed to other languages. I was doted on by my relatives for being fluent in Nyishi and I would proudly wear my flair for the language as a badge of honour. Not anymore. Today I struggle to hold a decent conversation in my native tongue, often using words in Hindi or English as a desperate crutch to complete a sentence. I have grown complacent. And so has almost the entire young generation of my state. We have developed a collective amnesia, an amnesia of the language, knowledge and worldview of our ancestors, a thread to our sacred past.

In 2019, I participated in a project that worked on the documentation and description of the Hrusso Aka Language. The Hrusso Aka community are natives of West Kameng District of Arunachal Pradesh. According to the 2011 census, the total population of the Aka community stands at around 8,100, and like most communities in Arunachal the number of native speakers can be estimated at less than the total population. Unfortunately, even this small number is dwindling. This phenomenon is widespread and observed across districts. The situation is alarming, especially since some of the indigenous languages are on the verge of extinction. It was during the time spent learning in a documentation project that I realized how endangered languages like Hrusso Aka could also die soon.

Spread across an enviable geographic area of 83,743 sq. km, Arunachal Pradesh has 26 tribes and more than 100 sub-tribes with as many languages spoken. Naturally a link language was due in order to bridge communication between the various tribes and also with 'outsiders'. To understand the development and the impact of a link language or lingua franca on indigenous languages, it is important to trace Arunachal's unique history within the Indian national framework.

Administration and reorganisation of Arunachal

Prior to Indian Independence the administration of the hill region of what is today Arunachal Pradesh was regulated under the Bengal Eastern Frontier Regulation Act, 1873, of the British colonial government. Soon after Independence in 1947, this region was reorganized as the North Eastern Frontier Agency (NEFA) with its administrative headquarters in Shillong. It was administered by the Ministry of External Affairs with the Governor of Assam as the acting Agent. NEFA was granted the status of a union territory in 1972, subsequently attaining full-fledged statehood as Arunachal Pradesh in 1987.

According to Dr Verrier Elwin, renowned anthropologist and Advisor to the Governor of Assam, NEFA was considered a country for tribal people with their indigenous art, culture and religion mostly untouched by other cultural systems. Due to limited contact, there was little influence from Hindus, Christians, Buddhists and non-Buddhists in the region. The tribes were left largely untouched because of the British policy of exclusion and non-interference. This policy actually served as a tool to protect British commercial interests by preventing British subjects (Indians) from travelling and trading in the region, thus insulating the indigenous people of the region from the wider world for a long time. Between the tribes themselves interaction was limited because of the indigenous communities' autonomous and independent existence. As such, the development of a lingua franca amongst the indigenous communities took a backseat and did not catalyse until a much later period.

The indigenous communities co-existed in the contiguous hill space. As need arose, some communities engaged in economic exchange. Along the way they learnt and adopted the basic and operational terms of each other's languages to get by, as is evident in the folklore of the communities. However, Assamese, the dominant language of the neighbouring Ahom kingdom, came to gain currency among those groups who engaged in frequent exchanges with the border communities of Assam. Arunachal shares an extensive border with Assam and over time the transactions between people across territories became regular business. People would endure long, arduous treks downhill just to buy a few essential goods from Assam. In fact, it is not uncommon to find village elders in remote villages of the state speaking in Assamese, recalling 'those days' of Diju Bazar, Harmutty and Dolohat Bazars. When the need for a lingua franca arose Assamese organically filled this space.

Even though Arunachal has a large pool of indigenous languages with some mutual intelligibility between tribes, a lingua franca still could not emerge from within. The advent of government administration and the introduction of the formal education system broke the mutual isolation of the tribes in Arunachal. The modern politico-economic system ushered in an ecosystem of co-dependence and tribes began associating amongst themselves and with those from other states for political, economic and administrative purposes.

In the absence of a common intelligible language, Assamese, English and Hindi emerged as link languages. Nefamese, a pidgin of Assamese language, was widely spoken. Nefamese takes its name from NEFA and Assamese. It played a crucial role in bridging the communication gap between the communities of Arunachal and Assam, and facilitated trade and administration in the region. During the NEFA administration, Assamese was made a part of the academic curriculum in schools. There emerged a literate generation of Arunachali students who grew up speaking and writing Assamese. Quite a few well known Assamese writers of Arunachal provide evidence of this: Lummer Dai, Tagang Taki and Yeshi Dorjee Thongchi are held in high regard for their contribution to Assamese literature. However, with Arunachal attaining statehood in 1987 and the subsequent adoption of the National Council of Educational Research and Training (NCERT) curriculum under the centrally governed state education system, Assamese was sidelined from the school curriculums. This, coupled with the arrival of non-Assamese speaking teachers, government employees, traders, business people and labourers in the state, paved the path for the growth of Hindi as a link language With Hindi gaining currency among younger and older generations alike, it has taken over Nefamese as the primary link language. Today, Arunachal is the only state in the northeast region of India where Hindi has acquired the role of a lingua franca. It is as noteworthy as it is unimaginable, because of the strong antagonistic views in other northeast states towards Hindi as a hegemonic linguistic imposition.

The language shift in Arunachal

In 2018 Prime Minister Narendra Modi remarked during his rally address in Itanagar, 'If you travel to Arunachal Pradesh for a day, you will hear more *Jai Hinds* than you would hear after travelling the country for a week,' and 'If there is any state in the northeast that speaks and understands Hindi, it is my Arunachal.' He even congratulated the youth for their grasp of Hindi. While people's command over Hindi is laudable, one needs to pause and ponder on this linguistic transition, and consider whether this proficiency in Hindi has been achieved at the cost of the indigenous languages.

It is understandable that in a multilingual state like Arunachal Pradesh with over a hundred languages spoken, there are practical challenges to assigning the status of lingua franca to any one tribal language. Due to active processes towards cultural integration of Arunachal within the Indian nation-state Hindi has emerged as the dominant mode of communication, whether it is in the administrative, socio-cultural or political sphere. In fact, knowing Hindi has contributed to socio-political and economic advantages and accumulation of cultural capital as against non-Hindi speaking communities. On the downside, the extensive proliferation of Hindi as the state lingua franca has impacted the usage and viability of primary indigenous languages. It has been observed that there is a rapid language shift towards the use of Hindi in both public and private spaces. This shift is apparent in popular media with an increasing number of local films, music videos and documentaries being produced in 'Arunachali Hindi', a local adaptation of Hindi. It is in fashion with Nagamese, a pidgin Assamese spoken by the Nagas. Hindi is gradually becoming the language of cinema, from delivering dialogues on screen to directing and managing the production crew on set. Unlike Nagamese, an increasing number of families in Arunachal are resorting to this Arunachali Hindi over their mother tongue, even in private spaces. Amongst the young generation it has taken over as the preferred language over one's indigenous tongue even within the same community. This phenomenon is acutely visible in the urban setup. An unintended consequence of this shift has been the endangerment of indigenous languages, as young people, who are the future of society, are all but forgetting their languages and the number of knowledgeable elders is quickly decreasing.

The way forward

At this rate, if necessary measures are not implemented soon, the demise of our languages and the unique worldview that they present seems imminent. Fortunately, there are some notables who have risen to the occasion and are working towards the preservation and continuity of our intangible heritage. As a case in point, the Hrusso Aka language under the Endangered Language Documentation Project is being documented and described by its community members with the help of researchers and experts. For the last three training workshops, Training and Resources for Indigenous Community Linguists (TRICL) have been encouraging and equipping the community linguists in the preservation of their respective languages. Some indigenous artists too have produced commendable work in their respective languages. Films such as the *Crossing Bridges* by Sange Dorjee Thongdok, *Those Songs and Lullabies I Used to Sing* by Kombong Darang, *Ho Delo*, a music video by David Angu to name a few, have creatively used their respective languages for such artistic expressions. While some artists like Taba Chake are making music in indigenous languages, others are allowing people to sneak a peek into the unique worldview through expressive sketches of folklore. The oral literature of the communities is also being published in local languages. As much as written literature is important, the revival of our indigenous art of storytelling is equally important. Delung Padung, a folk music artist, has been engaged in conducting plays based on local folklore in villages.

At the institutional level, the state's Department of Education is planning for compulsory inclusion of indigenous languages in the academic curriculum. A long-awaited action in the absence of written literature of most of the endangered indigenous languages is refreshing. However, according to the policy, only the native language of that region is to be taught in schools. This begs an important question to policy makers and civil society. What happens in a heterogeneous community, especially in an urban setting? Is it justified to deny the rights of students to learn their native languages for being schooled in a non-native region? This inadvertently champions one language over the other, most often the dominant language. The dangers of a language being marginalized are constant. We have to be conscious in our efforts to not let the cycle of language endangerment continue by giving space for the dominance of one language over others. As responsible citizens and stakeholders, let us not forget to speak our own while we speak the languages of others, and most importantly let us remain connected to our roots while we continue to branch. Hopefully, with our collective efforts we will be able to reverse the endangered status of our languages.

The Sun

OMILI BORANG

The sun poured itself
in generosity
Galloping over all that
stood in its way,
Only atoms could cut
through it
Seeping in between
the shining rays.
Here, the sun isn't merely a light,
It ought to be a reflection
A reflection of one's might
Of one's heart,
One's mind, one's sight.

They tell me it is dark
The way our future
leads,
But my sun is pouring out

Shining bright in all
my deeds.
So, how is it possible
That I bring darkness
when I arrive?
For I am my burning halo,
And my sun within
has thrived.

From the Jungle Series

BHANU TATAK

The Spectre Dentist

MILLO ANKHA

The knot in my chest was slowly growing. I rolled down the windows of my car. Despite its indifference, the city was alluring. It was the summer of 2015, and the sky was overcast. Soft, golden streaks cut across it now and again and the sprightly Gulmohar burst open gleefully and embellished the pavements. The towering concrete structures popped out of the earth soaring into the sky, the azaan permeated the silence with pigeons fluttering in the distance. My thoughts drifted, rising up like a smokescreen.

I caught the driver staring at me in the rearview mirror. He must have sensed the knot in my chest, or perhaps he simply wasn't used to seeing a face like mine. I had, however, become quite used to the way people stared at me, although it didn't seem to matter to them that it made me uncomfortable or anxious. When people ask me where my home is, like a trained parrot I spill the words out – Ziro, Arunachal Pradesh – words that sound hollow even to me and excoriate my insides.

Twenty-five years had gone by. I was done with my studies and had briefly practised dentistry for two years, I wasn't convinced about my choice of profession yet. Holding the degree was a strain on me to fit into a world I knew little of. But it made sense to move to a place where no one needed to stare at me for anything.

What was home going to be like? My mind was like an empty slate, unruffled. All I felt was, home was a conflict that each one of us carried, sometimes without realizing it or simply being in denial.

For almost seven years, my body was wired and weathered with the pleasant Bangalore air. It didn't occur to me how seasons marinated one's being. The seasons were something I had experienced and felt through the words and lamentations of writers and poets deep in their transcendence. During my idleness, waiting for patients to drop by the clinic, I found myself living in the pages of books. I would go tilling the red hardened earth, sow the seeds of hope, shred out the seeds of doubt, pray for rain, embrace and reap the harvest.

My narrative of myself alternated with all that was happening outside: the concerns of finding a ride back home, eating my meals, retiring for the night, waking up the next morning and turning up to face the sterile air of the clinic where every surface was swabbed with spirit and the demand for utmost cleanliness making me chary of things even in general.

Being present and tending to numerous patients left me bereft of energy and spirit. A feeling of being lulled shrouded me for days. My vacant eyes plumbed my being elsewhere, but in the sterile, walled chambers only a looming void stared back at me.

When my mother called me on one such day I had become quiet and volatile, breaking down at the slightest prompts from home. 'It will be a change of scene from the city, plus it is always good to come back to your roots. The cities are a facade and we'll never fit in there. We'll book your tickets okay, just come home…' My mother's words touched my swollen heart and I decided to pack my books and clothes and my file of degree certificates.

At Naharlagun, I was received by my parents and my younger sister whom I call Anga, meaning baby. She was studying in class X in a private school. My father was posted in a quaint town called Pasighat which was a six hours drive from Naharlagun, so it was just Anga and I in the house when the parents were out of town.

When we came back from a two week getaway in Pasighat an old friend of my father whom I called Aku, uncle, was looking for someone to assist him and take charge of his clinic in his absence. On a regular day he was employed in the health department, but as it turned out, he was also in the middle of building a house in his home village of Ziro. After going through my certificates and a brief interview Aku hired me.

I was introduced to his wife—I called her Atta—who had been assisting and maintaining the clinic ever since Aku had opened his private practice. I also met Yassung, the assistant-cum-receptionist, who was also from Ziro. At this point Atta joked that this clinic was now officially run by Apatanis.

The clinic was twelve years old. It was on the first floor of a building which stood between a traffic junction and a road turning in to the Medical line. An old metal board with a faded 'DENTAL CLINIC' hung outside the railings of a balcony equally rusty and weather-beaten with sun and rain.

It was a humble set-up with a single dental chair near one window. Instruments were arranged neatly in trays and materials lined on the shelf. The doctor's desk was placed near the other window, opposite a small bookshelf with dental journals and reference books. A half glass door with white laced curtains separated the working area from the waiting room. In the waiting room an old TV was mounted above the reception desk and in the corner a cheap china vase of plastic flowers was the only decor placed beside a wooden rhinoceros memento received from an organisation. The medicines, toothpastes, gels and syrup bottles were on display on the uppermost shelf. Adjacent to it a plain clock hung on the wall ticking away every second.

I stepped out on to the balcony to get some air and watched life on the road. The thin carpeting of the tarmac had leached off exposing the earth like an open wound. A stream of cars honked impatiently in the traffic, bikers meandered through the gaps, the traffic cop in his white, body hugging uniform abandoned his stand and was at the tea stall jabbering away and smoking cigarettes. Shops lined either side of the road and a row of pharmacies stretched towards the Medical line. In the evenings people swarmed like flies around the street food carts. The jagged mountains stretched into the horizon, guarding the town like a fort. At the end of the day, after calculating the accounts and entering records we turned off the motors, switched off the lights, closed the clinic, pulled down the shutters and locked it before leaving for home. I decided to commute by walking; the distance was do-able, plus the place wasn't as stretched and complicated as the big cities were. Besides, no one would be bothered by the way I looked or walked or breathed. What a relief!

December

In the cold of December I was now wearing turtlenecks and socks to the clinic. The silt in the air got sucked into the lungs if one stepped out without a mask or a scarf to cover the nose and mouth. Aku and Atta were away in Ziro for almost a month; their house was almost ready and soon to be completed. Taking charge of the clinic at this time I became confident in my white apron – doing and developing the x-rays, diagnosing the problem, recording impressions of the bite, fixing appointments, prescribing medicines and making daily entries in the record book. I had even picked up on my Arunachali Hindi, which was heavily doused with my south Indian accent. I spoke slowly, conscious of my diction.

Little children escorted by their parents came with loose teeth, mustering courage by praying before getting onto the dental seat, men and women with heavy swollen faces irritably complained of sleepless nights, one patient wanted to fill the gaps between his teeth, another wanted a permanent solution to brighten his teeth and there were those who patiently sat through their root canal treatments. Slowly, their apprehensions flowed into my hands as I carefully carried through the necessary procedures. Their breath warmed my gloved hands and my head bowed towards them –with my mouth mask on, my eyes fixed and held in focus by the halogen light illuminating my field of vision.

When patients asked for Aku I would tell them he wouldn't be back till maybe after the New Year. Some of them stayed to chat; some agreed to put their trust in my competence. On some days when there were no patients I went back to my solitary reading, letting my thoughts wander. Sometimes I felt the urge to write about things in general and I began scribbling, so much so that sometimes I was compelled to tear a sheet from the prescription pad. Meanwhile, Yassung would be embroidering gales, the woven wrap skirt worn by women, and cross stitching the traditional Apatani fisheye motif on the ties meant for her brothers. In her company, sipping chai, I listened to her stories about her childhood in Ziro and was transported to a familiar place that was nothing like hers.

After work walking became a devoted act I looked forward to. The route was through the main market of the town. During these walks, free of the clinic's attire and stripped of my identity I became invisible, and considering myself an outsider I simply became an observer, soaking in every detail with great curiosity. The more I walked, the more I felt alive. I began to think deeply about matters that seemed to have hovered around me – my past, the present and the future. When I felt that my mind was lost, my body planted itself on the ground, reclaiming the mind and the spirit.

Days turned to months and during this time I was subconsciously chronicling seasons too. The scudding clouds became my companions. When it rained I felt the water seep in between my toes bringing the mud and the slush of some forsaken path and depositing it on my feet. On sunny days I would be sweating bullets with damp arm pits; the roads were dry and dusty and the tropical heat made me thirsty and cranky (this was the only time when autos became my choice). I had waited for the winter patiently after the lashing rain and heat. Winter complemented my pensiveness. Fog cloaked the town. The mountains peeping through the building tops seemed to be teasing me about my choice of moving back, but I was pacified by the stillness around me.

I continued to walk, undeterred; I even got myself better walking shoes. My pace became swifter and lighter, my breath at ease and in tune with the steps. I became aware of my body, the beat of my heart, the flow of blood in my veins. Like the tides of a secluded sea, my thoughts ebbed and flowed. At times, distracted, I would slow down and observe people from a distance – a man piggy backing his aged old mother in the Medical line, a frail woman with the canula inserted in her hand, a circle of auto-rickshaw men smacking down their playing cards onto the centre where a pool of money was lying. The owners of thatched shops that displayed beads, bamboo hats, daos and trinkets of different tribes sprawled on the floor awaiting customers. The smell of the roasted corn wafted in the air and women in the vegetable market stuffed handfuls of rice in their mouths from the plantain wrappings. Green leafy veggies and orange peels carpeted this side of the road. It hit me that there was a need of decent footpaths for persistent pedestrians like me. There was not a single footpath anywhere. Why? I shrugged, thinking I was merely an eye probing around day in and day out, losing track of time, but these street images remained vivid and coherent in my memory for a long time.

During this phase, at night when the town lights were dimmed I would settle down at my desk at home, next to the window. The mountains weren't visible, but stars had appeared, floating afar, the rustling of bamboo leaves filled the valley and with my thoughts welling up in this melancholic air I would scribble on the paper what would spill out of me:

I have learned to witness my own life like the snail trails. Each step vanished and swept by my own skin and slug. I took time as it came, didn't try to compress it or omit it. So the sloppy rains, dreaded hot afternoons, winter gloom became my thing. I wrote, listened to songs I had never heard before, stared at the birds perched on the hibiscus bushes, the dogs soaking up the sun streaming from the swaying bamboo, the steam of the chai eventually giving up, the books collecting dust, the mirrors losing their clarity, those long walks wrapped up behind me each fold as I stepped on the soil that collected stories of every foot that has walked upon it. Solitude was intimidating because I came face to face with nothing else but a world in me, covered with the shell.

The day when the chief minister and his government fell in a sudden political development, I was wrapping up to go home for lunch and to be back after, when some boys came to inform us about an impending strike. They asked us to pull down the shutters and suggested keeping the clinic closed. I immediately called Aku to inform him about the situation. 'Should we be worried about the clinic?' I asked.

Aku told us to down the shutters and take the day off. The winter sun was in hiding, the shops were shut or shutting, the streets were deserted, and every corner was being combed free of humans. The strays wandered and the leaves rustled, whispering of the impending doom.

The State was riled up. Facebook and WhatsApp were flooded with news of the disgraced chief minister, the tug-of-war of the constituencies splashed across the news headlines – 'Murder of Democracy,' or a 'need', 'Arunachal Pradesh Crisis'. The drama behind the closed doors of the Assembly building left the viewers amused. VIP convoys loudly cried out the importance of their rush with blaring sirens. Everything had been shut for a few days because of the volatile situation. My mother called me to tell me not to go out on the streets but to stay home until things subsided and normalcy returned. After a lull of a few days when the shops opened again, I called Yassung and told her that we would resume our business. When we reached the clinic we found stones lined up in the corridor. Agitated, Yassung and I collected these stones in a yellow sack and carried it down to the road, dumping it right back where it had been brought from. 'Saala, why don't they clear the mess when they're done,' she fumed.

In the following weeks President's Rule was imposed on the state. Battalions of the Central Reserve Police Force, CRPF, had been deployed like fresh beans off the store, and they planted themselves in the markets and the streets armed with riot gear and shields and helmets and batons. It was harrowing to be on the streets in broad daylight. My indifference became incipient. Looking at their guns slung on their arms, I thought, when can I go walking by myself without these human fences? Can President's Rule bring the footpaths?

Around this time the Board examinations were approaching. My sister Anga's tuitions had picked up. She started coming to the clinic to study Hindi which was her weakest subject. In between patients, during the hours of translation and explaining Sant Kabir and Mirabai's dohas, I wondered what use these could be to a girl of an impressionable age, what use were they to me? Intrigued, I asked her what else was being taught. Was there any mention of the tribes or their culture and the history of our region?

Why was the region not heard of, or spoken about more often? Who was responsible for the indifference of people towards the region? For that matter I, myself, was ignorant and had slipped into the cloak of a step-sister. Why did it bother me now?

For long the remoteness of the place had held me back from approaching the region. No profound writers' words or thoughts of any native thinker galvanised me. The revolt within had metastasised and I wanted a form of solace and understanding of life and the world. I could no longer go on like this, being complacent about things and believing that some things would move on. What more did I look forward to? I couldn't say it was the world outside, but the monologues in my head were more interesting and I wanted to dig deeper. Things had altered, torn asunder by my own questions. I wanted to find out how the world inside me would respond to the world outside. Would it merge somewhere?

The distant horizon was blurred in twilight. The mountains were swallowed up in the dark. A few men outside the shops warmed themselves by the fire lit with cardboard cartons and plastic boxes. A huge dust cloud lifted up at our face; Anga and I had our mouth masks on. In the nebulous zone we were drifting towards Home.

Waves of Irony

TUNUNG TABING

(Translated from Hindi by the author)

The universe is a big ocean
Where waves of irony come and go
Every second, every minute shows
A new colour
Every colour seems extraordinary
Every phase seems surprising
The deeper you go
The uncountable jolt getting stronger
Sometimes the rays of the sun
Bring hope of light in life,
Then sometimes
They bring unease to someone's life
Sometimes drizzling drops of rain
Brings greenery in lives

Then sometimes it comes in the form of floods
And destroys life.

Firstly, by giving substantial meaning
Teaches pride to form
Thereupon writing an end of that page
causes people to suffer.

Somewhere, sometime,
Writing colourful pages
Filled with the rainbow of happiness
Then somewhere on blank pages
Only a cloud of sadness.
But both the pages belong
To that open, endless book
Of unending questions
Whose answers lie nowhere.

As much as I think about,
This creation of the creator
It gets more and more interesting
And then suddenly, rising in my mind
Rising waves of irony.

Among the Voices in the Dark

PONUNG ERING ANGU

My mind was winding in and out, between consciousness and dreams…my eyelids drooped while I struggled to keep awake as the car raced through the night, with the speedometer showing 100, 120 kilometres on the dark highway, the headlights focusing on the road and trees that seemed to have a life of their own.

Shadowy figures with crooked bodies silently raced with me, fading into the inky darkness that swallowed them up one by one. This was when a bandh, a sort of strike and closure, had been declared in the Dhemaji and Silapathar districts of Assam and I had to journey back by road, alone with my driver, risking everything, you could well imagine, at that time of the night.

It was deep into the night…or rather a very early dawn, and I wished for nothing more than to be tucked up in my bed. Wistfully I looked at the dim lights on either side of the road as we passed through a settlement and I yearned to rest, to crash into a death-like sleep on a warm and comfortable bed.

The lights of the burning lamps escaping from between the slender spaces of the thatched huts created a sort of ribbed glow and sparked off in me those memories of a time long gone when I was posted as a teacher in a place where there was no electricity, and where we had to walk for three, sometimes four hours, all uphill after crossing a giddily swaying bridge. Yes, it was in Bameng, a remote place in East Kameng, a far flung district in the mountains of Arunachal Pradesh. It was a nondescript hamlet then, when I was posted as a junior teacher in the High School and my husband was serving there as an administrative officer. A beautiful tiny place, Bameng seemed perpetually wrapped in a thick cloak of mist in the early and late hours of the day, followed by a deathly silence at 7pm when everyone retired to bed because there was nowhere to go and nothing else to do in the dark and cold surroundings.

I always felt I was atop the clouds floating in some wonderland. A sort of a fairytale-like place which made me somewhat homesick in the evenings with the kerosene lamps winking at me like glowworms in the dark, as nightfall descended on the plateau.

In those days there was no electricity and to top that, we had to walk up a steep incline to reach the town from a point called Pakke Point. The point could be reached from the main road after crossing a swinging, hanging bridge made of wire and wooden planks over a swiftly flowing Pakke river.

When I had my first encounter with the bridge I sort of froze. I could barely move and nearly passed out staring at the swift river coursing beneath, which could be seen between the gaps in the planks. I refused to move in spite of my husband's cajoling and pulling at my hands. I was holding on tightly to the railing of the bridge as if my life depended on it and screaming with my heart in my mouth.

Later, I would shut my eyes tightly and hurry across the bridge clutching the railings on both sides (yes, it was that narrow) yelling to any passers-by to stop till I had crossed. The reason being, the bridge moved more if there was another person walking on it besides me.

The school was a small one with scarcely 200 students studying in varying capacities till class 10. The children there were very innocent and receptive to new ideas and notions and I recall having an affectionate and friendly relationship with all my students.

There was this girl who was in class VI, let's call her Yelam, a plain looking girl who would have been lost among the sea of faces, if it hadn't been for that one black incident which happened that fateful afternoon. I was taking the English language class when all of a sudden some men burst into the classroom and began dragging away a girl, whom I later came to know as Yelam.

In spite of my protests and beseeching, they didn't listen and she was carried away crying for help. I had felt a gut-wrenching anger and frustration build up inside of me.... I couldn't do anything, I was so helpless. No one had come to the help of the poor defenceless girl. They told me that she had been sold as a bride to a man who was nearly her father's age.

This came under the purview of the customary tribal laws and traditions, so nothing could be done. It was only four years later that I met her again in my house, as a runaway. She was being taken to Seppa, the headquarters of the district, where her trial was supposed to be held. My husband told me that she was being kept in our house because there was no other proper place to keep her for the night as there was no separate cell for women in the jail there.

I wouldn't have known it was her, if she hadn't told me, and if our cook hadn't expressed his fears that the girl was maybe trying to do something drastic to herself.

'There are blood spots in the room madam. I am scared she might just kill herself,' he anxiously told me. 'She has been crying ever since she came and hasn't had a morsel to eat. Please talk to her. Maybe she will listen to you.'

So we got talking.

Yelam asked me if I remembered the moment she was dragged out of the classroom and carried away. When I replied that I did, she started shivering and a wave of sobbing overcame her. I let her have her catharsis and sat with her saying nothing, wanting to hug her but not knowing what to do, holding her hands, just feeling with her….

She told me how she was beaten and starved because she refused to sleep with her husband who was her father's age. 'How could I accept him?' She sobbed. 'It was revolting and repulsive.'

'But you have an eight-month old baby girl whom you left behind when you ran away. How could you have left her?' I asked.

'She was never my child. I was forced to bear her and I hated it,' she replied with a vehemence that took me aback.

It was when she tried running away that she was caught and bound with a log clamped around her legs and raped not only by her husband, but others too. It was barbaric and my heart went out to the poor suffering girl.

'What about your parents? Couldn't they do anything?'

'How can they? They are too poor to pay back the bride price they took from them. It's better to die than live this life of hell,' she said. 'If they send me back, I will kill myself.'

After her child was born they had let her be free as she had pretended to be resigned to her fate. But deep in her heart she never gave up. She had resolved to escape from that living hell. During that time she had met a boy who started to like her, and feeling sorry for her he had agreed to help her make her escape.

'What happened to him?' I asked.

'They caught us and beat him up. I do not know what happened after that. It's my fault that I took him along. I should have done it on my own,' she sadly told me. 'It's better to die than live this life of hell. If they send me back, I will kill myself,' she repeated, and sobbed softly.

'It will be fine,' I tried to reassure her, 'The administrative people are humans too and they will surely help you. They will understand.' I tried to sound convincing, but deep down I knew what the decree would turn out to be.

She knew it too, but we both wished for a miracle to happen.

We both pretended that everything would be fine and we chit-chatted on other subjects avoiding the uncomfortable ones and had our dinner in the glow of the firelight beside the hearth, deep in our own thoughts.

The next day she left with the police after I coaxed her into having some food. She thanked me, avoiding my eyes. I knew what she was feeling and why she did that. She didn't want me to see it in her eyes…the desperation, the utter dejection and raw fear that I could feel and sense in her being.

Two days later I came to know that Yelam had hanged

herself with a torn bed sheet from the ceiling fan in the PI's—
Political Interpreter's—house.

The verdict had gone against her.

I remember looking down at the darkness and the stillness
that had flooded the deep valley below from the official
residence, clenching my fists, not knowing what to do, a lump
forming in my throat and tears welling up and threatening to
fall, feeling a deep sense of loss and sheer frustration. A hoard
of memories both sweet and bittersweet lie buried there and
I am sure they resound in the nights when the fog and the
silence cloak the hills and the mountains.

When the babble of the brook breaks the silence in the
dark, and the cold wind moans through the cold wintery
nights, you will find my spirit there...lost somewhere, among
the voices in the dark.

A Ballad of the Adi Tribe

ING PERME

In Adi society one can study almost all aspects of folk literature including folktales, folksongs, ballads, legends, folk craft, sayings, proverbs, riddles, and folk medicine. This rich body of work helps us understand the social, religious, political and cultural life of the Adi people. It also plays a pivotal role and serves as a link to connect the Adi people with classical Adi literature. This folk literature is present in an unstructured way in the form of verbal lore that is passed orally and informally from generation to generation. Folklore experts are, however, declining. In the present context the Penge tradition is a dying practice and like the fate of folklore in many parts of the world, Adi folklore is also on the verge of extinction.

Adi folk literature can be divided into four broad categories: ballads, folk songs, folk tales and proverbs, sayings and riddles.

All these are contained in oral expressions. Adi ballads are narrative in nature and are presented in different styles. Penge, for example, is unique. It is the Adi tradition of singing to express grief and penge is a dirge, a song of lament. It reflects the Adi culture and is completely related to a person's physical and spiritual life. There are differences of opinion regarding the origin of Penge. In *Folk Culture and Oral Literature From North-East India*, S. K. Ghosh says, 'Penge originated from the death of Kari Bote and Toro Boro. The brave family members of Kari Bote and Toro Boro had organized a condolence meeting where people paid tributes in their names by highlighting their past activities and tried to console the grieving family with songs in the form of Penge. Since that time, when a person dies, the priest sings songs – penge – around the dead body.'[1]

However, in an interview Kado Apum described the origin thus: 'Tani was grieving at the death of Karpung and Karduk. As the couple were childless, Tani buried them and performed all the rituals. After the burial, both Tungi Taabe, a shaman priest and *penge ngelen* – meaning the penge – found a collective voice, and from that day penge originated.'[2] In the literature of the Adi Abang a miri or priest is known as Taabe. A professional penge singer is called Tungi Taabe or Isi Taabe. Since the Penge tradition *penge ngelen* originated with the burial of Tungi Taabe when breath became words – a professional Penge singer is now called Tungi Taabe to differentiate him from the more common term of shaman priest Taabe or Miri.

Penge culture still exists in Adi society. The penge dirge is of two types: *doban* and *penge*. In the former, a widow or widower or family members remember the dead person and lament their bad luck. Doban can be sung by anyone while expressing the pain of losing loved ones. No expert is hired.

For the traditional penge, however a penge miri is invited to mourn for the dead. The miri sings penge before the burial ceremony. It is sung in remembrance of the life of the dead person, who is considered to have lived through all of life's stages. Thus it is not performed in the event of the death of an infant or a young person. Traditionally, a penge performance is subject to strict conditions. The language of the traditional penge art form is very typical and not easy to understand, but it needs no translation as people respond to it naturally. Professionals who sing penge bring out the intimate grief with fascinating wordplay and the lamenting voice often moves the gathering to tears. It is found that even the penge professional sometimes cannot control his tears as he sings the ballads. Penge is performed throughout the night and it is organized only in the case of the natural death of a person, never for an unnatural death. No musical instruments are used.

Anybody can sing ponung, the festival dance songs, but not penge. Sometimes even persons who have the knowledge hesitate to sing penge. Singing penge is a sacred ritual, and only the brave choose to do it. According to tradition the miri escorts the soul of the dead person to the other world after death. Adis believe that only brave souls can sing this song of lamentation. It is also believed that the singer needs to sing the song carefully for if any kind of mistake occurs then a misfortune may happen in the life of the priest. As the Adi saying goes, '*Luba mamilo arei anyo lupa sudung*',[3] it is like inviting misfortune.

It is customary and compulsory to gift precious beads to the miri who performs the penge. Adis believe that there is life in the beads and the soul rests in them. Because of this belief beads are used in soul related rituals. Adis have faith that malevolent spirits are scared of beads. This is best expressed in proverbs like the one below:

Kuro nammar e tok-tik nako
Kuli nammir e tik-tak nako[4]

Kuro and Kuli are two precious male beads. The smell of these beads petrifies the malevolent spirits. Thus beads are meant to protect the priest from bad energy or malevolent spirits. Male or female beads can be given to the priest depending on the kinds of beads the family of the dead person has in their possession. If these are *mime tadok* (female beads) then four beads known as *dokpun abak* are presented to the priest. If they are *milokong tadok* (male beads) then the requirement is for one bead known as *apong atel*. Some people tie the beads with *ridin*[5] thread to a weaving implement called a *maksong sumpa*.[6] The *sumpa* must be made of the wood of the Tamak tree.[7] People call the *maksong sumpa* the beads and *ridin* as *ayit jumkeng*, translated as an amulet, a kind of *raksha kawach*. The miri priest keeps this as a weapon to fight malevolent spirit known as *banji-banmang*. The bereaved family also offers a new *badu*, a woven blanket made of cotton that the miri uses as a mat.

Among the Adi Padam it is customary to hire a penge miri to perform the funeral hymns, but in the Adi Minyong custom senior family members from the deceased family can also recite the penge. There are differences in presenting it though. For example among the Adi Padam people express their sorrow and pain by chanting, *ada tai yai*, while in Adi Minyong the chanting is *aya yaya yaya ulo lolo*. Both expressions are used for things that we cannot get back. They signify mortality or impermanence and the irreversibility of death. Another difference between the Adi Padam and Minyong society is that the *penge bedang*, the imaginary journey to the borders of Adi land, is chanted by the Padam whereas the Minyong do not sing it. The penge performance is very long. People call it *ladum larum abang*, meaning a the mixture of all ballads because the epic narratives of seasons and festivals like Binyat, Ekop, Doni-Dongor Abang are also included in the penge. In fact, the Doni Dongor Abang is a compulsory addition in order to trace the origin of Tani, the first man on earth, and the mythical stories behind how death came to man so that the mythical and remembrance of the different phases of life of the person who has died can be sung together as the shaman miri's soul starts the spiritual journey with the departed soul. The starting point of the journey is dependent on the home place of the deceased person. If the person is from the plains like Mebo, Ayeng or Pasighat then the penge bedang, literally the penge-road or journey will start from the plains towards the mountains, ending at a point known as Dodek Ngelek.

Presently this place is situated towards Karko in the Upper Siang District of Arunachal Pradesh. If the deceased is from the hilly regions then the penge journey will end towards the plain area called Motum Patang, presently situated at Motum village on the bank of Siang.[8] It is a belief among the Adi Padam that Dodek Ngelek is the last destination up to where the miri can guide the deceased. After reaching this destination the miri will tell the deceased to go on to his or her own world and express happiness for them although he is unable to accompany them any further. He has to return to the living world. The miri reminds them that their ancestors are waiting to receive them with open arms, and tells them to also let go of material clothes and wear clothes like their deceased ancestors. The miri further explains that they should not worry about their family members' life on earth. This is expressed in the Penge as,

No ngite be ne bom bi soge / No taying lapyo e dayon dakla
Ngite giling em tubit dakla / Poro gejong em tukok dakla
Ngite dodek e ngelek so / Poro dosing e maping dola
Ngite no ki e o bulu / Poro nibang e o bulu
E na ngite yapgo em morik du na / Doni basi e yimo nam em
Ngite no ki e o bulu / Doni galuk em pitkut pala
Sisik galuk em, ngite galuk em/ Pitlik bomkai
No ngite kardang e dasi pe / Poro lonmo em singka langka[9]

Dodek Ngelek is an imaginary place situated after crossing the Pasu Dino mountain, where departed ancestors practise agricultural work. Adis refer to it as *uyu ke lang Tani ke risu e*, meaning the border between the living and the dead where the soul crosses over to the other world. According to penge narratives from Pasu Dino, the soul of miri transforms into an eagle and flies back to the house of the departed soul from where he had started his journey. In penge it is described as,

Ngo isi tabe bote ngo / Lido yapgo em tikap sudakku
Nyumpong yapgo em/ Ngite yapgo em
Mokap supala / Pasu dino e
Banji ki-ki e nobo kope
Banmang ki-ki e nobo kope
Miding lapbung em bumo sudakla
Doni beying e si gi dan pe
Midi miyang e jajang dakku
Doni ane gumin lo isi tabe
Tabe dosing em maping doku[10]

The miri has treated the departed soul as a human being and escorted them on their spiritual journey, and it is Adi belief that if the miri does not then transform himself into an eagle the departed soul may follow him and return with him. Adi people consider the eagle as *banji-banmang* (a powerful malevolent spirit), and they have faith that an eagle would frighten the dead soul and stop him from following the miri. The immortality of the soul is a prevalent idea of Adi society and in the penge the soul of man is addressed as *bayuk*, meaning to transform, signifying the transformation of the physical body into the released soul. It is expressed in Penge as,

> *Doni ane aji ko ne*
> *Dongore olo e yorne kone ai*
> *Pedi pe bayuk e bikai*[11]

Adis have a strong belief in the Donyi-polo among. Everyone aspires to go to this place when the body is no more. In order to fulfil this desire the penge singing ritual is passed down from one generation to the next. Under the guidance of the miri the departed soul is escorted from the mortal world to Donyi-polo among. The Adi believe that in this place the soul lives forever.

Notes

1. S. K. Ghosh, *Folk Culture And Oral Literature From North-East India*, page 181, ed. Tamo Mibang and Sarit K. Chaudhury.
2. Interview with Shri Kado Apum (Miri) at Sibuk village on 11.06.15.
3. Interview with Shri Pelyem Yirang at Ayeng Village on 2.5.19.

4. Anthony Perme. 'A study of beads among the Adi of lower Dibang valley district', M.Phil thesis, Roing, page 26.

5. Ridin is a sacred creeper believed to petrify malevolent spirits. It has socio-religious importance.

6. Maksong sumpa is a weaving tool (batten) made from the wood of the Tamak tree. The word 'mak-song' originates from Tamak. A Tamak sumpa is used as a protective weapon in rituals.

7. A Tamak tree is a tree of the Tar family, *Caryota Urens*.

8. Interview with Shri Nakmin Perme at Mebo on 7.8.19.

9. Ibid.

10. Ibid.

11. Oshong Ering, *Indigenous Faith and practice of the tribes of Arunachal Pradesh*, pp. 52-53, ed. M. C. Behera and S. K. Chaudhuri.

Lost Souls

SUBI TABA

And the worst part of our romance?
    we never broke up
    we never started
    we jumped right into the mid.

We never said I love you
    we never said I hate you
    we were so besotted with each other
    we forgot to make our promises.

So the continents parted our ways
    and we just watched ourselves disappear
    thin into the air of changing worlds
    till we could no longer define what we once had.

From: *Dear Bohemian Man,* 2015

Bards from the Dawn-lit Mountains

YATER NYOKIR

Situated in the lap of the Himalayas, Arunachal Pradesh is a unifying abode of diverse ethnic communities following their own distinct tongues and cultures. There are 26 major tribes and hundreds of sub tribes with more than 90 languages being spoken. But amidst this plurality, there is one common feature among all the communities, that is that they are great storytellers. Without any authorized script of their own, they preserved their stories of time in their memories and disseminated them through word of mouth. This is how they were passed down to subsequent generations. When they took the form of chants, the stories were narrated by shamans and rhapsodists in social gatherings and at occasions like birth, marriage and at death ceremonies. They were didactic in nature and were meant to teach collective beliefs.

When we talk about the literature of Arunachal Pradesh we mean both the oral and the written. Oral literature is a manifestation of folklore and comprises sayings, anecdotes and stories of the origin myths as well as stories of animals and the universe, and of human beliefs and customs. Written literature includes works of fiction, poetry, drama, short stories, in creative interaction with oral literatures. There is an organic relationship between oral and written literature.

The twentieth century brought written literature to Arunachal Pradesh. The embrace of modern education stirred the artistic zeal in a few fertile minds and after 1947 we began to see the writings of authors such as Tagang Taki, Lummer Dai, Y. D. Thongchi, Rinchin Norbu Moiba, Samuru Lunchang and Kensam Kenglam. They were the first generation of literary luminaries from Arunachal. Lummer Dai's debut novel *Pharor Xile Xile* (1961) could perhaps be considered the first novel of Arunachal Pradesh, written by an Arunachali.

Given the absence of a script, writers of that period faced considerable difficulty in expressing themselves. In those days, Assamese was the medium of instruction in schools and many chose it as their language of writing. Crossing the linguistic bar, these first generation writers, with their versatile and unique stories, made an important contribution in the growth of literature in Arunachal Pradesh.

Their works were reflections of social reality. They often looked to folklore as a source for their writing. They derived unique inspiration from orature, myth, folk belief and customs, and this finds expression in their writings. Thongchi, in *Sonam*, explores the traditions and customs of Brokpa society. Dai celebrated the ethos of Adi folk life in his novels *Pharor Xile Xile, Mon aru Mon, Prithivir Hanhi.*

The year 1972 was a turning point for language in Arunachal Pradesh. English and Hindi were introduced in schools. English became the medium of learning and Hindi became the lingua franca by gradually replacing Assamese. As a result, those writing in Assamese began to feel a disconnect with the reader and Assamese as a writing language began to disappear.

Meanwhile, the growth of education led to people becoming more curious about their history and identity. In 1978, the Arunachal Pradesh Freedom of Religion Act was passed and enacted for the protection and promotion of indigenous culture and faith. As a result, writing on anthropological issues made its appearance. Among the writers here are Tumpak Ete, Osong Ering, Bani Daggen, N. N. Osik, L. Khimhur and many others.

Since the introduction of English and Hindi in Arunachal a new generaton of writers has emerged. Jumsi Siram's *Aye-Aluk* (1993) is the first novel in Hindi by an indigenous writer from the state. Yumlam Tana's *The Man and the Tiger* (1999) and Mamang Dai's *The Legend of Pensam* (2006) registered the entry of Arunachali writers in the literary canon of English and Hindi and also helped to take Arunachali writings beyond the borders of the state.

Mamang Dai re-created the pre-historic past of Arunachal Pradesh in *The Legends of Pensam* and *Black Hills*. Jumsi Siram in his novel *Matmur Jamoh Gumnam Swantantri Senani* re-invented the history of the murder of Captain Noel Williamson leading the Anglo-Abor War of 1911.

In the contemporary scenario, reeling under the effect of globalization, all aspects of culture and tradition have seen dramatic changes, and a kind of cultural amnesia has resulted. People have begun to question the established equilibrium and have started to abandon age-old customs and traditions. The effects of globalization can also be seen in the shifts in the literary paradigm of Arunachal Pradesh. Oral literature has begun to disappear into a state of oblivion. This friction of globalization and tradition is reflected in the themes of identity crisis, bucolic nostalgia and confrontation of social issues in contemporary writings.

Mamang Dai bewails in *This Summer*

> …begging the forgiveness of butterflies,
> and beauty that we destroyed
> in our hunt for life.

Yumlam Tana addresses the issue of identity crisis thus:

> The book of maps
> says nothing about our lands and forest rights

In recent years a number of young, educated writers have taken their place on the literary scene. What differentiates them from the writers of the first generation is their willingness to experiment with new styles and genres. With their refreshing tales and unique temperament, they have established themselves in the global literary arena. Tai Tagung in his drama, *Lapiya,* intentionally employed Arunachali Hindi. This has brought the attention of linguists to the Hindi spoken in Arunachal Pradesh. Gumlat Maio's trilogy *Once Upon a Time in College* is a campus novel. Dai's *Stupid Cupid* can be described as chick lit.

Shaping the destiny of ethnic literature in recent times, there is also another body of writing coming up in indigenous languages. Some important names here are Takop Zirdo, Tony Koyu and Yabin Zirdo. There are also a number of Hindi poets and writers such as Taro Sindik, Jamuna Bini and Joram Yalam who have made a significant contribution to the progress of Hindi literature in Arunachal Pradesh.

The work of all writers, whether from the earlier generation, or more recently, draws on and confirms the continuity of the strength of myth and folklore in creative writing in Arunachal. Mamang Dai's anthology *The Balm of Time, River Poems*, Tana's *Man and the Tiger* and *Wind also Sings* and L. W. Bapu's *Khanduma's Curse* are the explicit assertion of the amalgamation of traditional literature and creativity.

The emergence of creative literature in Arunachal Pradesh is a relatively recent phenomenon. With a handful of writers it made its debut in the middle of the 20th century. Within this short journey the many awards and honours won by Arunachali writers speak of their versatility.

The Summit
Speaking to Tine Mena

MAMANG DAI

The northern frontier of Arunachal Pradesh is a remote, sparsely populated world of towering mountains, rivers and deep ravines. There are villages here, but for the most part they are cut off from the rest of the world with no road connectivity, no electricity, no visitors except for the occasional government official who usually appears once in a blue moon to oversee the boundaries of the nation in the far eastern Himalayan mountains of the Indo China border.

What would be the dreams of a young girl born in such a village? Hard to know. The landscape is awe-inspiring but there is little else here. Maybe one shop, the semblance of a school building with a dilapidated exterior, for who would want to study from books when surrounded by earth and sky and the beating rhythm of village life in tandem with the rhythm of the seasons?

Yet the lines of destiny can cross mountains and sky and reach out to touch a life in an unexpected way. Tine Mena from one such village, Echali, close to the international border in Arunachal's Dibang Valley

District, is the first woman of the state and of North East India to have climbed Mount Everest on 9 May 2011.

It has taken me a while to get to this interview. The years intervened. I saw Tine at the annual Reh Festival celebrations in Roing, headquarters of Lower Dibang Valley District. Reh is a significant festival of the Idu Mishmi and for the first time, the event was organized by an all-woman central Reh celebration committee in 2019. It was a grand, joyous affair. The finale was a fashion show that focused on the famous Idu textiles, with the full repertoire of fusion wear, music and young children in traditional dress. At the end, the showstoppers, Tine and her colleague Muri Linggi,[1] suddenly appeared, in mountain climbing gear, shashaying down the catwalk to the loud cheers of the audience. It was a great moment.

The interview idea resurfaced. So come the winter of 2019 I travelled to Roing to meet Tine with one question in mind:

All I wanted to know: How did it all happen?

Here is our conversation:

TM: I grew up in the mountains. When I was a young girl, I was a porter for the Indian Army patrolling the border outposts. Sometime in 2001 my uncle started the Athu-popu[2] Heritage Foundation to promote

---

[1] Muri Essomi Linggi of Roing, Lower Dibang Valley is the third woman from Arunachal Pradesh to conquer Mount Everest, reaching the summit on 14 April 2018. A mother of four, Muri Linggi was photographed at the peak holding a placard which read: 'Beti Bachao, Beti Padhao'.

[2] Athu-popu is a sacred place marked by a large rock standing alone at an altitude of some 3,500 metres situated at Kayala Pass on the India-China border. In Idu Mishmi belief this site is one of the resting places for the souls of the departed as they make their journey towards a new life.

adventure tours in the region. I knew the routes well from my experience as a porter for the army patrols. So I became a local guide. In 2007 some sportspersons from Manipur came here on a trekking expedition.

MD: Did they come as tourists?

TM: No, they were invited by the state government.[3]

TM: The trek to Athu-popu is very arduous. There were about sixty five of us in the group. Two days before reaching Athu-popu the boys in our group said there were only four kilograms of rice left. They suggested that maybe we should turn back. I was upset. After eight days of trekking it was wrong to turn back. I said, we have only so much rice left. What if I make *kitchdi?* Is this okay? We can reach our destination in this way. Everyone agreed. Later the local MLA [Member of the Legistative Assembly] heard about it. He was happy with my management and awarded me a one lakh rupee contract for road-cutting work.

MD: Where was this?

TM: It was on the same road to Athu-popu!

MD: I wonder, are you superstitious? What did you think of then, when you were at the summit? Did you think of gods, about Athu-popu; do you have a deep belief in something that gives you strength?

TM: Yes. I used to travel a lot with my father through the mountains and through jungles. And he used to always say, respect the big trees. If you cut a tree, tell the tree

---

[3] This was a trekking expedition to Kayala pass border area sponsored by the State Directorate of Youth Affairs and Sports and the Athu-popu Heritage Foundation in the winter of 2007.

why you are doing so, why it is necessary, if you need its help. And if you see a big river, never challenge it. You should never think – oh, that's nothing, I can cross it if I want. You must be humble with nature. That is what my father always said.

TM: I will tell you of an incident that happened before the Everest climb. In our belief Athu-popu is the route taken by dead souls to reach the other world. It is the bridge. Once I had two girls working with me, aged thirteen and fifteen. The younger girl was possessed by the spirit of someone who had died twenty five years ago. At night I would feel someone standing close by and sometimes I heard someone plucking leaves in the jungle. I felt this presence – on moonlit nights the dead have the power to take your soul, but sometimes a cloud comes in between. I said, if you have come to take someone's spirit, take mine. Why take this young girl, because I have also brought her here with a personal guarantee to her parents that she will be safe with me.

You may find it strange…but I could talk to this spirit who also communicated and said, 'Now I am going. This is my last night. I will meet you on the other side.'

When I was at home there was a bird that kept hopping about, up and down here and there…

MD: What kind of bird?

TM: It was (*pointing to the dots on the wooden beam*) a dark reddish brown.

MD: A big bird?

TM: No, it was a small bird. This was before my mother's death. In a dream the spirit said to me, I have come many times to meet you but you keep chasing me away. The spirit also said, in your place I will take someone else. Within three months my mother died. And that young girl, within a month, her father also passed away, and there were some more accidental deaths and people who were murdered. I don't know, I felt the spirit haunting us was a woman who had committed suicide twenty five years ago when she was pregnant.

So I believe in unseen powers. Never think that you are immune to any force. There will be a reaction. Anything can happen. There will be consequences.

MD: You have to have a strong heart to climb Everest.

TM: Oh yes, (*laughing*). You know when I was a porter for the army – I was, what, seventeen years old – I carried two dao – the traditional sword – I fished, I chopped wood. I did all sorts of things. Then during that trek I told you about, when I was working as a local guide I met expert climbers and people from our Sports Department. I met Meetei Sir[4] who told me that I needed to change my attitude and learn patience. He

---

[4] Dr Kangabam Romeo Meetei, In-Charge Adventure Cell, Department of Youth Affairs, Government of Arunachal Pradesh. A Manipuri officer, Dr Meetei has been instrumental in promoting adventure sports and mountaineering in the state and played a vital role in producing three Everesters from the state. A recipient of the State Excellence Award Dr Meetei led the successful Team Arunachal Mt Everest Expedition 2011, and created history by producing two women Everesters, Tine Mena, and Anshu Jamsenpa, who scaled Mt Everest twice in a span of 10 days. He has also led the first IMF (Indian Mountaineering Federation) Mt Gorichen Expedition at the Indo-China Border.

said that I needed to learn technique and improve, and then I might be a mountaineer!

So it happened that four of us – two boys and two girls – were called to the Sports Department. We had never been out of Roing, but two of us, Apali Lombo and I, turned up. We planned that we would become tour guides and set up a small shop and do business. Well, we were sent to Manipur MMT [Manipur Mountaineering Institute] under the aegis of the Manipur Mountaineering and Trekking Association, where various adventure and environmental and also eco-tourism activities and mountaineering trekking are conducted. I was selected as the best student, and Apali was best runner. Meetei Sir was happy and suggested we go for further basic training. It was September; we had landslides and road blocks and Apali couldn't make it, so I went alone for training at HMI [Himalayan Mountaineering Institute]. It was an international basic course and I won a gold medal as the best student. It was here I saw the documentary of Tenzing Norgay.[5] My interest was aroused. Now this was my aspiration. When I returned from HMI Meetei Sir asked me, 'Tine, now what do you want to do?' And I said, 'I want to try to climb Everest.'

Meetei Sir was supportive. He told me to start preparing while he looked at different courses that might help me. Acclimatisation courses were crucial.

---

[5] Sherpa Tenzing Norgay: Everest veteran Tenzing Norgay and Sir Edmund Hillary reached the summit of Everest on 29 May 1953, becoming the first people to stand atop the world's highest mountain.

Finally I was selected as the representative from Arunachal Pradesh for a pre-Everest course with the Assam Mountaineering Association.

Our first expedition was to the Jawahar Institute of Mountaineering and Winter Sports [JIM&WS] in Pahalgam, Jammu and Kashmir. I found climbing 6,000 metres was not a problem. I felt a good rapport here and opted for the advanced course. In 2010 I made an attempt to climb Shivaling in the Garhwal Himalaya, but we couldn't make it. I was trying to build up my climbing technique for Everest. Also, another climber was suffering snow blindness so I had to go and rescue him. The Assam Everest expedition was scheduled for 2014, but now I felt ready for Everest and I wanted to start as soon as possible.

The problem was how to finance an expedition. It was very difficult for me to raise fifteen to twenty lakhs. I needed sponsors. So I turned to the government, met the chief minister, MLAs and government officials. Everyone was encouraging and ready to donate. But I also worked, collected wages – *hazira!* (*laughing*).

MD: What kind of hazira?

TM: Stones, trucks, small contract works, stone chipping…

MD: Really!

TM: Well, work is work. There is a wholesale place some eight kilometres from here for broom grass selling at rupees three a kilo, so I rode a bike, got a whole bunch and started selling for rupees five. (*laughing some more*). I also sold vegetables, kopi – bitter berries – and whatnot. From my side I managed to raise approximately one lakh thirty thousand. Lots of people read about the proposed Everest expedition and offered a thousand to ten thousand and up to a lakh of rupees in donations. The deputy commissioner also raised an amount of more than two lakh for me through Housie draws! The bulk of the funding was from Jindal Power Ltd [JPL][6] with a sum of fifteen lakh. It was 2011, and now everything was rushing ahead. Two months before the expedition I decided to arrange my father's wedding.

MD: A wedding?

TM: Yes. My mother passed away in 2010. As the eldest in the family I was still observing a lot of taboos – food restrictions – even during my stay at HMI. Now I felt responsible for my father. You know, mountains are beautiful, but they are dangerous. One mistake and the mountain will take your life. I worried about my father. I was leaving him. Maybe I would not return. He was almost sixty years old. I thought if I don't make it back there should be someone to look after my father. And even if I came back I was a woman and might get married and leave him. My father should have someone in the house.

MD: How did your father respond?

TM: My father has always encouraged me. In the matter of remarrying, I pressured him a bit (*laughing*). Maybe I got him a bit drunk too! Then I left for Nepal. At least my mind was free. If tomorrow I am no longer alive

---

[6] Jindal Power Ltd (JPL) has undertaken three hydro power projects of more than 5,000 MW capacity in Arunachal Pradesh, the 3,097 MW Etalin project (near Tine's home village of Echali), the 680 MW Attunli project and the 1,600 MW project at middle Subansiri.

at least my father would have someone to take care of him and look after the home.

MD: What was the feedback you got from people at the time, about your wanting to climb Everest?

TM: Oh it was negative and positive. Some people said, why spend so much money when there are so many mountains here? Why can't you climb here? How to reply? I know there are mountains here but these mountains and Mount Everest – there is a difference – I knew I couldn't explain it to them until I had made a record and came back a winner. So I didn't say anything. Other people said, okay, just climb and come back!

On the 1st of April 2011 the expedition was flagged off by Arunachal Governor General (Retd) J. J. Singh. Another colleague, Anshu Jamsenpa,[7] was also with me. We had planned to start together but in the end I went ahead to Delhi. I had some six lakh with me, and in Delhi I received the money from the Jindal Group. Now I had to really prepare. Equipment was expensive. In Kathmandu I went to second hand shops to buy foot gear and dungarees. What's with old, I thought. This will be fine.

There was paper work – I had to fill in applications. I am illiterate, but young people helped me. On the 7th of April we were at Lukla Everest base camp. Meetei

_____

[7] Anshu Jamsenpa: Born in Dirang, West Kameng, Anshu Jamsenpa, a mother of two, scaled Everest twice in 2011 on 12 May and 21 May. In 2017 Anshu broke the record for the fastest double ascent of Everest by a woman, in five days, on 16 May and 21 May.

Sir accompanied us till this point. Anshu Jamsenpa arrived five days later. In the meanwhile I did my own 'boil food' cooking and got on well with our guides. At this time I felt some problems. It was to do with acclimatisation. Everything was moving so fast. I felt the loss of my mother but Meetei Sir encouraged me. Go ahead, he told me. Your mother used to say, 'do something!'

On the 6th of May I had reached camp 2. The weather had been bad during this time but we heard the Everest route is open, so my Sherpa guide and I had planned to aim straight for the summit skipping camp 1. Weather conditions were still bad, but I thought, this is quite natural in these parts. My guide also said, if you feel you can, we can attempt it. We were low on oxygen and if we went ahead and failed to reach the summit and returned, we would not have oxygen for a second attempt. My guide had already prepared Camp 3. So I thought, live or die I have to try. This is what I have come for. To climb this mountain.

On the 6th of May we left camp 2. There were very strong gales and everyone was against going ahead. We had to halt one night at camp 4, taking shelter near the tent of Apa Sherpa who has climbed Everest so many times. On the 8th my guide and I decided to start for the summit. It was 8 pm when we left. No one was around. Now you see traffic in these mountains, but at that time, a decade ago, there was no one. In fact we felt like ghosts wandering in a dream – no walkie-talkies, no food, no medicine. The Nepal authorities telephoned our department group and told them that my Sherpa guide and I had left, and that if anything happened it might not be possible for us to make it back.

But there was a lull in the weather. On the 9th of May at 10.15 am we reached the summit.

MD: What did you feel?

TM: I've done it! My guide and I boiled some water and ate a half packet of Maggi. All the food was finished. We left the other half there on the mountain. You will see this in my video. Yes, you feel a sense of power and great energy. It was after great effort, but if you focus on what you want you will have success. All kinds of thoughts crossed my mind. I missed my mother. I really missed my mother.

MD: I am sure your mother must have seen you.

TM: Yes, maybe. It was like a dream. What will happen now? What will my life be like now? These were my thoughts as we made the descent.

We are sitting on a low bench facing each other. Through the open door sunlight pours in and I can see the tall trunks of big, green trees. Tine shows me some photos but says she lost many documents when her house caught fire some years ago. Her new place in Roing is a spacious, traditional house with a raised veranda in a forested hill by the Eze river. Tine is the eldest of seventeen siblings. Only two of them survived, Tine and her younger sister, who is outside with Tine's little son. Tine and her husband, Pronov Mega, run the Mishmi Hills Trekking Company started in 2013 to promote adventure tourism, trekking, rafting and artificial outdoor wall climbing. Tine tells me that they have had the occasional Everesters meet, twelve in Arunachal Pradesh, to discuss mountain climbing. Considering the congestion in the Himalayan climbing scene today they feel that the number of climbers should be limited, and climbing can be rotated between well known and unnamed peaks. One final question: I wonder what Tine feels about the big dams in Arunachal Pradesh.

TM: I don't know what to think. Big dams, yes, there is development – roads and electricity – but I have seen it and know for a fact that once the land is touched it is changed forever and we can never get the trees and forests and rivers back.

MD: I saw, in one picture, you were wearing a traditional muffler on the summit of Everest.

TM: Yes, (*laughing*) I left it there, on Everest.

Notes on Contributors

AYINAM ERING is Assistant Professor of Hindi in Government Model College Geku, Upper Siang District in Arunachal Pradesh. She completed her post-graduation in 2012 from Rajiv Gandhi University. She has also served as guest faculty at the Institute of Distance Education, Rajiv Gandhi University, Itanagar.

BHANU TATAK is an artist based in Roing in Arunachal Pradesh. A sociology graduate from Miranda house, Delhi University, Bhanu has participated in various exhibitions and curated several spaces for artists to come together and has been active on ground since 2016. Having participated in the India Art Fair 2018, Arunachal Literature and Art Festival 2018 and 2019, Pangsau Pass International Festival 2020, Bhanu is now more focused on curating spaces where she can paint and recreate the meanings of her paintings. Currently she is painting from her personal studio with the aim of withdrawing from the public and painting for herself alone and not for exhibitions.

CHASOOM BOSAI is a student of Literature and a graduate from the University of Calcutta. She is currently preparing for the Arunachal Pradesh Public Civil Service examinations. She has done an advanced photography course from Light and Shadow Institute, Kolkata. She is a passionate poet and has often been published in Delhi Poetry Slam e-magazines. She loves travelling, reading books and is a foodie.

DOIRANGSI KRI is from Tezu, Lohit district in Arunachal Pradesh. She is the author of two books, *A conversation book of Kaman and Taroan Mishmi* and *Kutemba: The Legend of Lohit Valley*. She served as an assistant teacher under the Sarva Shiksha Abhiyan from 2006 to 2010. She has a Masters in English Literature from Rajiv Gandhi University, Arunachal and has many 'firsts' to her credit including being the first Mishmi assistant professor from Lohit and Anjaw district. Currently, she is at the Department of English, Indira Gandhi Government College, Tezu and is active in many seminars and conferences. She is a recipient of the SORUM PUL award for academic achievement, instituted by the Cultural and Literary Society of Mishmi.

GEDAK ANGU is an M.Phil scholar at the Arunachal Institute of Tribal Studies at Rajiv Gandhi University. He did his Masters in English Literature from Rajiv Gandhi University. He also worked as guest faculty at Tadar Taniang Government College, Nyapin and Government Model College, Basar. Writing poetry is a medium of expression for him but painting also works for him. He also considers planting and gardening as therapeutic for his personal growth.

GYATI T. M. AMPI is an Apatani writer/poet from Ziro, Arunachal Pradesh. She is the author of two books, *Will Spring Bloom Again?* and *An Undying Dream – Musings of a Decade.*

She finds solace and tries to spread little smiles and love in this mundane world through her works.

ING PERME is assistant professor in the Department of Hindi at Jawaharlal Nehru College Pasighat, Arunachal Pradesh. She belongs to the Adi tribe and is currently doing doctoral research at Rajiv Gandhi University. She is a folk literature enthusiast and has published research articles and participated in conferences at home and abroad. She is bibliophile and asthete and has previously worked as a general announcer and newsreader in Hindi for Prasar Bharti Pasighat and Itanagar.

JAMUNA BINI is from Ziro, Arunachal Pradesh. She is a gold medallist in Hindi. She writes in Hindi and in her mother tongue Nyishi. Her writings include literary criticism, travelogues, short stories and poetry. Her poems are included in the M. A. Curriculum of Allahabad University and her recent book of Nyishi folktales, *Uiimok*, features in the NCERT curriculum in government schools in Rajasthan. Her works have been translated into several Indian languages including Santhali, Assamese, Malayalam, Punjabi, Rajasthani, and also into Turkish. Currently she teaches at Rajiv Gandhi University, Arunachal Pradesh.

KARRY PADU, an independent filmmaker, was born in Aalo in West Siang District. She runs 'The Vivid Project', which sheds light on issues such as racism, politics, religion and gender equality in Arunachal Pradesh. Her film 'I am Property' explores polygamy and impunity in the context of customary laws in the state. She is the Director of Wild Flower Production based in Itanagar and is involved in various social activities, the most prominent being the Arunachal Literature and Art Festival and the latest edition of Yomgo River Festival at Aalo. She lives in Itanagar.

KOLPI DAI, born 1995 in Sikang, Arunachal Pradesh, has been writing poems since she was in the eighth grade. In 2014 she joined the B.Sc course in the college of Horticulture, Pasighat, and has been writing for the college magazine. She has received a number of prizes for various regional poetry elocution and local competitions. Her interests revolve around science fiction, the laws of nature, philosophy and the fight against social evils. A young writer, Kolpi aspires to add to her understanding and perspective to be able to add value to her work.

LEKI THUNGON (LEKI WANGMO THUNGON) is currently a Ph.D candidate in Anthropology at McGill University. She was an assistant professor of Sociology at Lady Shri Ram College, University of Delhi, and Ambedkar University, Delhi. Her training in Literature, Sociology, and Social Anthropology shaped her approach toward gender, justice, memory, and violence. Her life has been split between New Delhi and what she calls 'backhome' (Arunachal Pradesh). This reflects in her perspective on identity and the politics of storytelling, which attempts to go beyond the simplistic binary of mainstream and marginalized.

MAMANG DAI is a poet and novelist. A former journalist, she has worked with WWF in the Eastern Himalaya Biodiversity Hotspots programme. Her first book, *Arunachal Pradesh: The Hidden Land*, received the State Verrier Elwin Prize. She is a recipient of the Padma Shri (Literature & Education) and the Sahitya Akademi Award. She currently lives in Itanagar, Arunachal Pradesh.

MILLO ANKHA is a former dentist who turned to photography and writing as a form of self-expression. As a diaspora child she takes an interest in understanding and documenting her native landscape with a distinct gaze. She engages with mixed media art, farming and takes long walks when she's not occupied with work. She prefers picnics over writing any day.

MISHIMBU MIRI belongs to the Idu Mishmi tribe from Dibang Valley. She has a Masters from Rajiv Gandhi University Roni (Rono) Hills and now works as District Food and Civil Supplies Officer for the Government of Arunachal Pradesh. She has been researching shamanic rituals, folklore and folk tales, as well as children's stories and rhymes of different tribes. She has written a book on Idu hymns as well as a book for children and is a keen trekker, photographer and rafter.

NELLIE N. MANPOONG is a journalist with Arunachal Times and is based in Itanagar. She won the V. Ravindran Excellence in Journalism Award (print media) twice in the gender issues category (2014) and in the politics and governance category (2019). She was awarded the state gold medal in 2020 by the governor for her contribution to journalism. She is also the first convenor for the gender council of the Arunachal Pradesh Union of Working Journalists.

NGURANG REENA is a first-generation feminist, writer, researcher, educator and an activist from a Nyishi Tribe community in Arunachal Pradesh. She was teaching as an assistant professor at Miranda House in Delhi University until she quit her job in 2018 to seek the truth of her father's mysterious death. She has been vocal against human rights violations in the country, primarily in the North East region and her writings/interviews have been featured in both national and international news channels and media portals. She is the co-founder of Ngurang Learning Institute, a non-profit working towards empowering women of Arunachal, and a recipient of the Zubaan-Sasakawa Research Grants for Journalists.

NOMI MAGA GUMRO is a teacher and home maker who has recently published a collection of her poems in Hindi. For her, poetry is always a revelation, an emotional upsurge, an expression of creativity and imagination, and a way to speak of her untold feelings. Her life experiences animate much of her poetry and she derives inspiration from interaction with others.

OMILI BORANG graduated from Delhi University and is currently studying at the Daying Ering College of Teacher Education in her home town Pasighat, Arunachal Pradesh. Omili first started her writing journey as a columnist for a local daily, *Eastern Sentinel*. She is the founder of MUR'ENG (meaning rainbow in the local Adi dialect), a platform encouraging and supporting local artists and talents. She aspires to become an educator and help in making quality education accessible in her state.

PONUNG ERING ANGU was born and brought up in Pasighat and has written and self-published four books as a hobby. She graduated from Jawaharlal Nehru College, Pasighat and completed her post-graduate degree from Punjab University, Chandigarh. She is Joint Director in the Department of Women and Child Development, Government of Arunachal Pradesh.

REBOM BELO, is a Ph.D scholar in Hindi at Rajiv Gandhi University. Born in 1992 Rebom is from Yomcha, West Siang District.

RINCHIN CHODEN is a doodle artist currently based in Itanagar. She describes her journey into the art world as a therapeutic method of coping with the pressures of the modern world. Her artwork varies between cartoon depictions of her everyday struggles to detailed pieces on culture and tradition. Her inspiration comes from the subtle nuances of everyday life. She prefers wrapping up her days with a warm cup of tea and the snuggly company of her cats.

RONNIE NIDO is an independent researcher and aspiring writer who prefers the pronouns she/her. She is passionate about writing her gender and brewing cups of green tea, both equally critical. She received her formal training in criminal justice social work from the Tata Institute of Social Sciences, Mumbai. Her areas of focus include local governance, gender justice, victimology and criminal reforms. She has previously been associated with Zubaan Publishers as a young researcher under the Zubaan-Sasakawa Research grant in 2018. She is currently based in Itanagar and is completing a fellowship with the Government of Arunachal Pradesh.

SAMY MOYONG is a neuro physiotherapist and lives in Pasighat, Arunachal's oldest town. Birthing poetry while her peers were birthing babies wasn't in her plan but she is glad poetry happened. Some of her early poems were self published in an anthology entitled *Echoes of the Heart*.

STUTI MAMEN LOWANG is a self-taught artist currently working as an assistant professor at the Department of English,

Visva-Bharati, Santiniketan. Her ongoing Ph.D thesis is on the exploration of ugliness as an aesthetics of resistance in the context of the contemporary Indian publishing scene. Disillusioned by the world of academia, which she feels is rife with all forms of discrimination, she looks forward to exploring the intersections of identity and mental health via the graphic storytelling format. Though she began drawing solely to overcome trauma, she now aims to share her experience and vision with the world.

SUBI TABA is an epiphany seeker, poet, writer and a Nyishi girl born in Seppa during the midsummer monsoon of 1989. She was awarded '100 Inspiring Authors of India Award' in 2018 for her debut poetry book, *Dear Bohemian Man*. She has a Master's degree in Agriculture from Nagaland University and now works as an Agriculture Development Officer in Arunachal Pradesh. She has performed her poetry in literary and poetry festivals. She loves time travel movies, exotic cuisines, wandering in the woods and being goofy with her little sister.

TAKHE MONI is mother to two children, and works at the Government Higher Secondary School, Itanagar. She has a keen interest in writing poetry and is an avid reader.

TINE MENA, born on 17 September 1986 in Echali, a remote village just 28kms from the last Indo Tibetan Border Force outpost in Upper Dibang Valley, is a well known mountaineer. She became the first woman from the North East and Arunachal to scale Mount Everest on 9 May 2011. Tine lives in Roing, Dibang Valley where she and her husband run the Mishmi Hills Trekking Company.

TOKO ANU was formerly editor at the Indian Cultural Forum, New Delhi. She currently works as a Circle Officer in Arunachal Pradesh. She received her Master of Philosophy degree in Sociology from Christ University and has also worked as guest faculty at Mount Carmel College, Bengaluru. Apart from writing, she is a fitness enthusiast and enjoys long walks in nature.

TOLUM CHUMCHUM is completing her Masters in Business Administration from Rajiv Gandhi University, and is also a keen poet. Her works have been published in various places and she is a member of the Arunachal Pradesh Literary Society.

TONGAM RINA is a journalist based in Arunachal Pradesh and chiefly reports and writes analyses on a number of issues ranging fron gender to justice, hydropower to the dilemmas of environment, governance and development. Besides her work as the Deputy Editor of the *Arunachal Times*, Tongam spends her time travelling, teaching and reminiscing on life and change. The backdrop of the North East of India and Arunachal in particular, serve as the inspiration for her work and support to causes.

TUNUNG TABING is Assistant Professor, IDE, Rajiv Gandhi University, Rono Hills, Doimukh, Arunachal Pradesh. She is currently working on a doctoral degree from the Hindi Department of Rajiv Gandhi University. She is interested in field poetry, story writing, translation and hosting.

YANIAM CHUKHU is a student researcher from Arunanchal Pradesh. Her interests include indigenous language, culture and folklore.

YATER NYOKIR is from Pasighat and is a scholar, translator and book reviewer. She has published a number of research papers and has also translated the works of contemporary Arunachali writers into English. She is an active member of the Arunachal Pradesh Literary Society and is currently doing her M.Ed from Rajiv Gandhi University, Doimukh.

Glossary

Abu	Brother or parallel cousin in the Sherdukpen language
Aka Chandu	Younger/youngest paternal uncle in the Sherdukpen language. Chandu means the youngest in the family.
Aka	Paternal uncle, also used for maternal aunt's husband, in the Sherdukpen language.
Anu	A generic term for sister or daughter in the Sherdukpen language. In terms of kinship terminology, it is often used to refer to girls and women who are sisters in relation, thus the term highlights the rules of incest and matrimony.
Appa	Mother in the Nyishi tongue
Azang	Mother's brother or paternal aunt's husband in the Sherdukpen language.
Azu	Sister-in-law, cross cousin, any girl or woman who is not a sister by relation in the Sherdukpen language.
Bukhari	A wood-based heater
Chura	Fermented cheese
Daayan, boksi	Witch in Hindi and Nepali respectively
Hung ja	Butter tea
Jabrang	Schezuan seeds
Jhumkheti	Slash and burn farming

Kakung	Dried flattened maize
Namda	Traditional bamboo house of the Nyishi tribe of Arunachal Pradesh
Phurup	Farmhouse
Rimboches	Honorific term for an abbot of Tibetan Buddhist monasteries
Tamul	Betelnut